MURDER IN THE SAND

Inn Vermont Cozy Mysteries, Book 5

THEA CAMBERT

Summer Prescott Books Publishing

Copyright 2021 Summer Prescott Books

All Rights Reserved. No part of this publication nor any of the information herein may be quoted from, nor reproduced, in any form, including but not limited to: printing, scanning, photocopying, or any other printed, digital, or audio formats, without prior express written consent of the copyright holder.

**This book is a work of fiction. Any similarities to persons, living or dead, places of business, or situations past or present, is completely unintentional.

CHAPTER 1

Spring had finally arrived in Williamsbridge, Vermont—my hometown. What had begun as an unseasonably warm winter had ended with plenty of snow, beginning on Christmas Eve and running all the way through the end of March. By that time, most of the maple sugar Vermont is famous for had been tapped. The woods around the Inn at Pumpkin Hill were scattered with purple skunk cabbage, Dutchman's breeches, and trillium. The breezes that blew up and down our front porch smelled fresh and green. Mom and I—we run the inn together—opened the windows and tackled our annual spring cleaning, and by the beginning of May, the whole place was clean and organized and we were ready to transition into the summer season.

Williamsbridge is a very small town if you're counting locals, but the population swells regularly with the seasonal influxes of tourists. We're nestled into Vermont's Green Mountains and can offer brilliant fall foliage in the autumn, snowshoeing and ice fishing in the winter, fresh air, and maple sugar in the spring, and long, sunny days and hikes through the mountains in the summer. The town itself is quite historic. It was founded by William Hadley in 1763. Visitors always get a little chuckle when they find out we were literally named Williamsbridge because old William Hadley built a bridge over Cottontail Creek, which runs through town, and everybody found their way around the region based on that bridge. Things were "south of William's bridge" or "just past the creek, over William's bridge," and the name just stuck.

In the many years that have passed since those early days, the town has become a little jewel, shining in the valley, built around a town square, with pretty, bricked sidewalks, quaint shops and restaurants, a lovely park, good schools, and plenty to do, from getting out into the mountains for hikes, strolls, or picnics, to the many festivals and events the town hosts. I was already looking forward to summer's

Blueberry Festival, but that wouldn't come for a few months yet.

Since my family had been in the inn keeping business, which encompassed pretty much my entire childhood—and I was twenty-eight now—we always took a single week in late spring as a vacation. Well, when I say *vacation*, I use that term very loosely. We consider not running the inn to be a vacation. We might not take a trip to some exotic place or sleep in every day. Vacation to us meant downtime. Technically, I hadn't been on an actual trip for seven years, when I drove with some of my college friends to Boston for a weekend between undergrad and graduate school.

But this spring, I was packing my bags and driving to Maine to visit my cousin Rebecca—and to say that I was excited about it would be an understatement.

"Do you have plenty of sunscreen, Eloise?" Mom was sitting on my bed in my cottage, watching me pack. My cottage lies just behind the inn's main house, where the backyard meets the woods.

"Just one bottle. I'll only be gone for ten days, you know."

"Don't forget to pack a few nice things for going out in the evenings."

I smiled at her. "I won't."

"Doc and I will miss you."

"You would've missed me even if I'd stayed home. You'll be off on your own trip."

"True."

Mom lived in the main house with her husband, Doc. They were still technically newlyweds, since they'd married just before Christmas. "Doc" is Dr. Ian Jenkins. He's been our family doctor all my life. He grew up with my parents. My dad passed away several years ago and my mother was heartbroken. To have lost him when he was a hundred would've been painful, but he was so much younger—and Mom was only in her mid-fifties at the time. Then she was surprised by a second chance at love. Doc and my parents had gotten into all kinds of trouble and had all kinds of adventures together as kids, and I can honestly say that when Mom found herself in love with and marrying her old friend, I could sense my father's smile all the way from heaven.

After I finished earning my master's degree in journalism, I moved home to Williamsbridge and took a job at the local paper, the *Williamsbridge Onlooker*. I had rented my friend Edna's garage apartment and eked out a living, helping Mom out at the inn when I could. A while after Dad died, Mom invited me to become her partner—an opportunity I gladly took. The job came with the cozy caretaker's cottage and afforded me a very short commute to work—a walk across the backyard—and the chance to be near Mom but still maintain a measure of privacy. I still write and edit for the paper in addition to my inn keeping duties, and my two careers generally complement each other and keep me busy.

My editor, Walter, had given me the week off to go to Maine, and had promised me that everything was under control at the paper. Mom and Doc were headed off for a mini-vacation of their own. And Matthew Stewart, the third and final member of our staff at the inn, would be staying in Vermont to keep an eye on things and run the one thing we had opted to keep on the calendar—a murder mystery weekend event. We'd hosted our first murder mystery weekend the past fall, and it had been a huge success . . .

despite the fact that an actual murder had taken place in the village.

Matthew was more than just our handyman/superhero/jack-of-all-trades at the inn. He was a writer—had just had his first book published and was on deadline to finish the second. *And* he was my boyfriend. But before he'd been my boyfriend, he was my *best* friend. We'd grown up together in Williamsbridge, had chased through childhood, trudged through adolescence, and bloomed into adulthood side-by-side. At Christmas, we'd finally admitted that we had romantic feelings for one another and had cautiously started dating.

It's a funny thing—to date your best friend. It's like starting in the middle and the beginning at the same time. In some ways, we were like an old married couple, finishing each other's sentences, foreseeing each other's needs . . . But in other ways, we were brand new, and every touch of his hand, every stolen kiss brought a thrill, a blush, a flip of the heart. We wanted to protect our friendship, so we were moving slowly, and that was just fine with me. The only downside to my trip to Maine was that Matthew, knee-deep in writing, wouldn't be able to come as he had hoped to. And I would miss him terribly.

On the other hand, Matthew and I agreed that it might be a good thing that I was taking this trip to Maine on my own. It would be the first time I'd meet my cousin Rebecca. I'd grown up not knowing I even *had* a cousin, because back a few generations, when our great-grandparents' two sons, Robert and William, hadn't gotten along, Robert's branch of the Lewis family had moved east to Maine, while William's had stayed back in Vermont with the inn. The next couple of generations had never crossed paths until I got in touch with Rebecca, who frankly could've been my sister, we were so much alike. About the same age. Both journalists.

"You and Rebecca can have a girls' week this visit," Matthew had said after telling me he wouldn't be able to go with me. "You know, do all that girl stuff, like painting each other's toenails and such. I'll go next time." We were equally disappointed, but Matthew always looks for the positive, which was one of the reasons I love him.

I hadn't told him that yet, by the way—that I loved him. He knew I loved him as a friend, of course. But since the advent of our romance, we hadn't said the three magic words. We'd get around to it, I felt sure.

But I wanted to wait until the right time. I wanted to savor every step in our relationship.

Matthew hefted my bag into the back of my car—a jeep with the inn's logo on the side. "What have you got in there?" he said with a laugh. "Are you transporting gold bars or something?"

"It's probably the books," I said.

"How many books are you taking?"

"Oh, I don't know. Ten? Fifteen?"

"El, you're only going to be gone for ten days. Do you really think you'll have that much time to read?"

"No, but I have to have the right book for whatever mood I'm in."

"Don't you have an E-reader?"

"Oh, don't worry. I packed that too," I assured him.

"Now you drive safely," Mom said. She and Doc were standing on the driveway with Matthew and me. "Call me when you get to the hotel tonight. And again when you get to Maine tomorrow."

"You know I will." I was splitting the drive into two days even though it was only about a six-hour trip. I knew I wouldn't get off from home until afternoon because of loose ends I needed to tie up before leaving, so I'd booked a hotel for that night.

Rebecca and I were actually going to be staying on a small island off the coast, called Purple Finch Island. The island is named for its impressive population of migratory purple finches which populate it in the winter. Then in the summer, the finches leave, and the summer people arrive. It's an old, historic summer colony, reachable only by mail boat—which was another reason I would make the last leg of my trip the following day. The last mail boat would have already left by the time I reached the dock on the day of my departure.

Mom and Doc hugged me. "Have a wonderful time," Mom said.

"We'll have coffee at the Steamy Bean when you get back. I want to hear all about your adventure," Doc said with a smile. Doc and I have coffee together, just the two of us, once a week at our local coffee shop, and it's come to be a highlight of both our routines.

Mom took Doc's arm. "We'll let you two say goodbye," she said with a grin. "Eloise, be safe. And we'll see you in a week and a half."

"You have fun on your trip too," I said.

They went up the porch steps and into the inn, leaving Matthew and me alone in the gravel parking lot.

I looked up at our inn, at the wide front porch, the gardens, the picket fence, then down the hill to the town of Williamsbridge, with its tree-lined streets and quirky shops and restaurants already bustling with business for the day.

"Are you sure you're okay to run the murder mystery weekend alone?" I asked, taking Matthew's hand.

"Absolutely. We've done a few of them now and I've got the routine down pat. Besides, it's only for the weekend. After that, I'll be on vacation for a week too."

"Except you'll be working the whole time."

"But I love writing. I don't mind."

"Can't wait to see what you write," I said, looking up into his hazel eyes.

"And I can't wait to show you." He leaned down and kissed me tenderly, then pulled me in for a tight hug. "I'm going to miss you."

"I'll call you tonight."

"See that you do."

I climbed into the jeep and headed down the hill and out of town, feeling a rush of excitement as the road opened up before me.

CHAPTER 2

The Sleepytime Inn of Bauerstown, Maine, was like a blast from the past. I followed the signs and pulled into a covered drive next to the front office where I would check-in for the night. I'd crossed over the state line about an hour back and was relieved to have the bulk of my drive behind me. In the morning, I'd drive over to the coast, park in a secured lot, and catch the boat from Sea Star Bay to Purple Finch Island, where Rebecca was already checked in and waiting at the Hideaway House Inn.

The desk clerk at the Sleepytime gave me my key and a map of the property with my room circled in thick black marker. I was told to drive around to the back of the building and take the stairs to the second floor to find room twenty-seven. During my stay, I was welcome to use the pool and ice machines, and to enjoy the complimentary continental breakfast in the morning between the hours of seven and ten.

As I climbed the stairs with my heavy bag, I cursed myself for not narrowing down my book selection before leaving home. Matthew had probably been right about that. Thinking of him brought a smile as I pushed open the door to reveal a classic hotel room, with two full-sized beds, a television, a tiny closet, and a perfectly serviceable bathroom. The bathroom was done in tones of peach and featured a shell motif, from its shell-shaped sink to its many shell imprints in the tub/shower combo, to the shells featured in the wallpaper. A peek inside the nightstand drawer revealed the expected notepad, pen, and Bible. I could swear my parents and I had stayed in just such a hotel when I was about ten years old. I had been enchanted by the shell sink back then. Now, even if the décor wasn't quite to my taste, it did remind me that I was nearing the coast, so I was able to embrace the kitsch.

I opened my suitcase, chose a book, took a hot shower, and ordered a pizza. I put on my most comfortable sweats and snuggled up to wait for the delivery person and called Matthew.

"How was the drive?" he asked after we'd said our hellos.

"Smooth. No problems."

"Good."

"How's the inn? Did Carol and Stacey arrive yet?"

Carol and Stacey Blake, two globetrotting, mystery-solving sisters who'd come to our first murder mystery weekend—and had then given us a *very* favorable review on their extremely successful blog—were coming to Williamsbridge to participate and help out with our latest event. They'd been to every murder-mystery-solve-it-yourself in existence, and about a million people were glued to their social media accounts and reviews. This weekend, Carol, who'd become a close friend to me, had agreed to play the murder victim.

"They're all settled in their room," Matthew said.

"Did you give them the—"

"Gift card to the Duck and Pheasant? Yep."

"And did you leave the—"

"Flowers in their room? Yep."

"Good." I smiled into the phone. "How's the book coming?"

There was a pause. "I wrote for a couple hours this evening."

"But?"

"But what?"

"Pretty sure I heard a 'but' in your voice."

"I'm sure it's nothing," he said. "Just a touch of writer's block. I think the weekend will be a good distraction. Just need to clear my head."

"Sorry I'm not there to help."

"Well, you *are* my own personal muse."

"I meant with the murder mystery. You don't need any help writing that book."

Matthew laughed. "I expect I'll pull through just fine."

Matthew writes in the fantasy genre. His first book was quite an epic—the story of a lost dwarf who ends up befriending a wood nymph from another time and they help each other find their way home. The publisher contracted Matthew for a trilogy, and where he'd spent a good five years writing the first novel, he now had one to plot and produce the second in the series.

"Maybe the pressure of a looming deadline is part of the problem."

"No, I think a deadline is a good thing," said Matthew. "Someone needs to light a fire under me."

"Like that time I set your sock on fire in the fifth grade?"

"That was an accident. And those tube socks needed to go anyway."

We both laughed at the memory.

"I'd better go," I said, stifling a yawn. "I—" I stopped talking abruptly. I'd almost said it—almost said those three little words. They'd almost just rolled off my tongue like no big deal! "I ordered a pizza," I said.

"Ooh. Yum. Extra cheese?"

"Of course."

"Enjoy. And sleep well."

"I will. You, too."

"El?"

"Huh?"

There was a pause. "Talk to you tomorrow."

"Okay."

We hung up and I flopped back onto the bed. I collected all the pillows and propped them up behind me for maximum lounging comfort. I called Mom and told her I'd safely arrived at the hotel just before the pizza guy knocked on the door. I settled in with my hot, gooey pizza and flipped on the television to find that one of my favorite romantic comedies was on. A blanket of contentment settled over me as I bit into the first slice of pizza, and I never did get around to reading.

CHAPTER 3

I awoke the next morning when the sun came streaming through the gap between the drapes, sending a single sliver of light directly across my face. I blinked, confused for a moment about where I was. Then I smiled when I remembered. I got up, washed my face, put on a flowered skort, t-shirt, and sandals—the perfect summertime meet-your-cousin-for-the-first-time outfit—and pulled my hair up into a ponytail. Then I jogged over to the lobby, which had been transformed into a dining area complete with buffet and little flower arrangements on the scattering of small tables. I grabbed a bagel and tiny containers of cream cheese and jelly. While I waited for the bagel to pop from the toaster, I watched the other guests wandering in, some with children in tow.

There was a dad helping his daughter, who looked to be about four, pick out a tiny box of cereal from the rack, and a mom, feeding the baby a bottle while juggling her own breakfast. I smiled as I watched them, hoping I'd have a family of my own one day—even when the toddler threw a fit because the dad wouldn't let her have a chocolate-covered donut and when the mom nearly fell asleep in her own oatmeal, presumably after being awake with the baby for much of the night. I wondered how Matthew felt about children.

Within an hour of waking up, I was packed and checked out, handing in my room key as I drove past the office. It was a glorious day for a drive, and in only a few hours, I'd reached the coast and parked my car in the secure lot at Sea Star Bay. The lot attendant directed me to the boat launch nearby. I walked down a dock to a small ticket kiosk, where I paid for my ticket to Purple Finch Island and took a seat on the bench.

"You're lucky to be taking the first boat out this morning," the old gentleman in the kiosk had said. "You'll get to see the jumpers."

"Is that a kind of fish?"

The man smiled. "No, I mean the mail jumpers. You'll see."

When the mail boat—the *St. Huey III*—arrived at the dock, a group of five athletic-looking teenagers, all wearing red shirts, navy blue shorts and running shoes, climbed aboard along with me and the other passengers. I hadn't known what to expect when I found out I'd be taking a "mail boat" from the bay to the island, but the *St. Huey* was surprisingly nice, with an air conditioned cabin, comfortable seats, and plenty of windows. Within a very short time of leaving the bay, the captain pointed out Purple Finch Island, which lay just ahead.

Those of us who would be going ashore at the village were told to stay on board until the boat circled to the back of the island. Meanwhile, the *St. Huey* edged up to the shoreline and I was shocked to see that as we passed certain docks which jutted far out into the water, the teens took turns leaping off the bow, landing on a dock, running at top speed to a mailbox perched near the end, dropping off letters and parcels, and then running back and jumping onto the stern of the still-moving boat. The *St. Huey* barely even slowed down during this process, and the jumpers, upon landing, would breathlessly grab their next delivery and get back in line. What a fascinating way to spend your summer vacation! All of the other passengers—me included—cheered every time another delivery was successfully dispatched.

Finally, the *St. Huey* pulled into a dock on the far side of the island. I lugged my bag down the platform and to the grassy mainland. The tiny village of Kasko spread out from the pier, and just to the right was a utility vehicle with the words *Hideaway House Inn* painted on the side. My ride.

"Hello, I'm Eloise Lewis. I think you're here for me?" I said, dragging my bag along behind me.

"Well, hello, Miss Lewis! I'm Jane Gander," said the woman, who was tall and delicate to look at, with her long, straight, shiny hair and fine features—but who was strong as an ox beneath all that, as she grabbed my bag with one hand and hoisted it into the back of the car with very little effort. "Welcome to Purple Finch Island!"

As we drove through the village, Jane explained that *kasko* was a word from the Wabanaki people who'd originally settled in Maine. It meant *heron*, and indeed the coast saw the arrival of several varieties of heron each spring—the Great Blue Heron and the

Yellow- and Black-Crowned Night Herons among them. Jane pointed out restaurants, like the Briny Catch, the Lobster Pot, and Fish Tales. There were funky little shops, like Catch of the Day and Sea Glass. As I watched the town roll by from my window, I began to feel right at home. This was Maine's version of Williamsbridge! As we cleared the village, the land became more thickly forested with pine trees. We wove through the trees, and then I could see the rocky coast again, and just above it, shining in the late morning light, was Hideaway House. It was glorious—painted in shades of white and gray with a decidedly Victorian architectural flair and surrounded by sumptuous gardens.

"Wow. It's beautiful—and huge. How many rooms do you have?" My inner innkeeper had a million questions.

"Twenty-three," said Jane, pulling into her reserved parking spot. "Plus, there's the great room—it's in this building here. This is where you'll check-in. It's like a huge, shared living room with a fireplace, gift shop, and café. There's even a lending library in there, so you can borrow all the books you want during your stay. And then there's the owner's cottage. Only the current owners—the Bryants—and their special guests stay there. This was actually once the summer home of a very wealthy family at the turn of the century."

"It's amazing."

"You'll have plenty of time to enjoy Hideaway House and all that Purple Finch Island has to offer. Oh, and your cousins are anxiously awaiting your arrival." She got out of the car and opened the back, then swung my bag out and set it down.

"Cousins? There are more than one of them?" I had only been expecting Rebecca.

"There are two," said Jane with a smile. "Oh—and there they are now." She pointed as the front doors of the inn opened and two young women came hurrying out. One was tall and thin, with dark, wavy hair like mine—Rebecca. I recognized her from photos we'd swapped. The other was short and curvy, with long blond hair and an enviable tan.

"Eloise?" said Rebecca. "I can't believe we're finally meeting!" She wrapped me in a warm hug.

"Rebecca! I'm so glad to be here!" My smile moved from her to the other cousin.

"This is my younger sister, Penny."

"So glad to meet you." There was a hug for me from Penny too. "Wow," she said, looking more closely at me. "You look more like Rebecca than I do! You two could definitely pass for sisters. And you're even both newspaper reporters. What are the odds?"

"I look like Dad. Penny looks like Mom," Rebecca explained, linking arms with me as we walked up the steps into the inn's lobby. "Your room is right next door to Penny and me, and we all have an amazing view of the water."

"And there are all kinds of fun things going on this week," said Penny. "Including an awesome music festival."

Rebecca laughed. "I just want to sit by the water and read all seventeen books I brought along."

I smiled at her. "I can tell we're going to get along just fine."

CHAPTER 4

Every room at Hideaway House had a name. I was staying in The Loft, and right next door, Rebecca and Penny were in The Sunset Suite. We were the only two guest rooms on the third floor of the inn and shared a balcony that looked out over the beautiful deep blue water surrounding Purple Finch Island. I laid my suitcase on the queen-sized bed, which was tucked up under the eave opposite a wall that featured a large window and the glass door that led out to the balcony. The bed was covered in a fluffy down comforter and had six luxurious feather pillows. It also had a quilt thrown across the bottom, the patchwork done in all the colors of the world outside the window: greens, blues, and snatches of deep cranberry red and gold.

To the right of the bed was a gas fireplace with a beautiful wood mantle draped in garlands of shells, and in the corner to the left was a lovely old armoire with a television housed inside. Opposite that there was a cushy couch where a second guest might sleep. There was also a small dressing area that opened into an equally small bathroom. It was cozy and quaint and made the seven-year wait for this vacation worth every single day.

I walked out onto the balcony and stood at the railing. After taking in the view, I closed my eyes and breathed in deeply, feeling the warm sun on my face. I could've stood there all day, but Rebecca and Penny would be waiting for me downstairs. We were having lunch in the little café on the grounds.

I reluctantly left the balcony, locked my room, and headed downstairs, where I found the girls already seated and looking at menus at an outdoor table in one of the gardens.

"I've died and gone to heaven," I said as I sat down.

"Isn't this place amazing?" said Rebecca. "We come here every year—we have since we were kids. This year Mom and Dad decided to go off on a cruise instead, and Penny wasn't sure she was coming until the last minute. But I'd never let anything get in the way of my annual week at Hideaway House."

"I don't blame you," I said. "So, you and the rest of the family live on the mainland?"

"Yes," said Penny. "We all live over on the other side of the bay, in Nettlestown, not far inland."

"Oh, right. I knew that," I said. "I saw the sign pointing toward it when I veered to Sea Star."

"You'll meet all of them eventually," said Rebecca. "We didn't want to foist the whole family on you all at once."

"I'll be looking forward to meeting Uncle George and Aunt Catherine," I said.

We ordered lobster rolls and crispy fries, along with the inn's specialty blueberry cake for dessert.

"We always start our summer stay here with lobster rolls," said Penny with a laugh. "Hey, you two will come to the music festival, right?"

I looked at Rebecca, and she quickly nodded. "The Purple Finch Folk Festival is this weekend. It's a big deal on the island every summer." She smiled fondly at her younger sister. "And this year, it'll be the best one ever."

Penny beamed.

"Why?" I asked, looking back and forth between them.

"Because Penny's band, The Vision, is one of the acts," said Rebecca.

"Wow, that's amazing!" I said. "You're in a band?"

"Yep," said Penny, taking out her phone and showing me a photo of four people, smiling for the camera with their arms around each other. There was Penny, right in the middle. To her left was a petite girl with long red hair, and to her right was a girl with gorgeous blond hair, holding up a pair of drumsticks, her free arm around a guy with matching blond hair and tan, holding a guitar. "Just a little group of friends. We've been performing together for years. Just small gigs, but it's fun. We weren't sure we were going to get it together in time for the festival, but it looks like it's going to work out." She waved her crossed fingers and smiled.

"I wouldn't miss a chance to hear you!" I said, and Penny looked very pleased.

"So, tell me more about your job at the newspaper in Williamsbridge," Rebecca said as the waitress poured lemonade all around.

"I love it," I said. "I do a lot of editing these days, but Walter, the managing editor and publisher, keeps me busy with news and features too."

I was dying to tell Rebecca about the other part of my work—the *Miss Smithers* column. "Miss Smithers" is our local advice columnist in Williamsbridge—and although no one knows it, she's me. Actually, I'm the fourth Miss Smithers. My good friend Edna—the one with the garage apartment I used to rent—was the third. Every now and then when I get too busy at the inn, Edna will still take the column for a spell, but I try to keep all my plates spinning most of the time. I'd already decided to keep the Miss Smithers column to myself, rather than tell Rebecca and Penny about it. I hadn't even told Matthew or Mom, and it felt wrong to tell anyone else. Besides, Walter would probably sense it if I did and fly over to Maine to have my hide.

"So . . ." said Penny, grinning, "is there anyone special in your life, Eloise?"

Rebecca looked at me and laughed. "If the huge smile spreading across your face is any indication, I'd say that's a yes."

"It is a yes," I affirmed. "His name is Matthew Stewart. He's my best friend *and* my boyfriend."

"Eloise, why haven't you mentioned this before?" said Rebecca, swatting me with her napkin.

"We started dating at Christmas. It's still new."

"Christmas was months ago!" said Penny. "Show us his picture—and don't even pretend like you don't have one with you, because we know you do."

I took out my phone, feeling my cheeks getting warm just thinking about my "boyfriend." Everyone back home knew by now that Matthew and I were an item. For that matter, half the town had apparently thought we'd been dating for years, since we were basically always together. This was the first time in recent memory that I'd been able to say that word —*boyfriend*. Is that what you call the person when you're both almost thirty? Were we past the boyfriend-girlfriend stage? Matthew seemed too young to be my *gentleman caller* . . . And I hoped I was too young to be his *lady friend*.

"Wow, what a hottie," said Penny, looking at a recent snapshot of Matthew I kept on my phone. I'd taken that picture just after Matthew had gotten into his old red truck and rolled down the window. He was smiling at me, sitting there in his usual baseball cap, his scruffy brown hair sticking out around the rim, his hazel eyes contrasting nicely with the red of the truck.

"So handsome!" said Rebecca. "Do you think he's the *One*?"

"Look," said Penny, pointing at me, "she's got that huge smile again! He's the *One*!"

"We'll see," I said. "I can definitely say that he's not *not* the One." I sighed. "More and more these days, I hope he is."

CHAPTER 5

"I'm definitely gaining five pounds on this trip," Rebecca said with a laugh that evening, as we sat at a cozy, candlelit table at the Crispy Cod, a little hole-in-the-wall restaurant right on the beach. The place looked modest from the outside but was clearly one of the most popular eateries on the island. There was a line a mile long for people without reservations, and no one seemed to mind the wait. The girls, and in fact the whole Maine branch of our family, were old friends of the owners and had called ahead to reserve us a table with a view.

I ordered a big bowl of the restaurant's signature cod chowder, a delectable, thick mixture of fresh fish, bacon, corn, potatoes, and cream. I snapped a photo of it and sent it to Edna, who had given up working at the newspaper several years back to pursue her life-long dream of owning a restaurant entirely devoted to soup, which she'd named Potbelly's. Rebecca took a bite of her lobster pie, which was topped with a buttery cracker crust, while Penny cracked into her steamed lobster and dipped the meat into butter sauce. We all ate in blissful silence for a few minutes.

"So, tell me more about your band, Penny," I finally said, wiping my mouth and then tearing off another piece of crusty bread to dip into my chowder.

"The Vision basically started out as the proverbial garage band, back in middle school. It was just me and my friend Hayley back then. She's the redhead in the photo I showed you. We'd always dreamed of performing, so we pulled together a few friends and have been at it ever since. I sing leads, Hayley is on keyboard, Rachel is our drummer, and Ken is our guitarist—but he didn't join the group until college."

"Ken's family actually owns Hideaway House," Rebecca put in. "That's where the girls met him."

"Oh. So is the woman who picked me up at the station—Jane—a relative of his?"

"No, she's the manager. The family comes and goes every summer."

"The girls and I came out here for a weekend getaway about five summers ago," said Penny. "The inn hosted a karaoke night and they liked us so much they invited us to do a poolside gig. Ken heard us play and came on board as our guitarist. That really took us up a notch." She smiled proudly. "In fact, we performed at the Songs of the South music competition in North Carolina last month, and we came in third."

"I've heard of that competition. That's amazing!" I said.

"That's why we were invited to take part in the Purple Finch Folk Festival this weekend. And that's an even bigger deal because a rep from Maine Tunes, the record label, is coming to hear us play."

"That's incredible! So, you could get a recording contract with them?"

"If Mr. Faber likes what he hears," said Penny. "Chip Faber. He's produced some of the greats."

"You must be so excited!"

"I am," said Penny, but her smile faded, and she looked down at the lobster on her plate.

"Penny, what is it?" asked Rebecca. "Something's been bothering you."

Penny chuckled. "Eloise, you might as well learn this now. You can't hide anything from this one." She put a hand on top of her sister's. "She can always tell when something's up, so don't bother trying to hide it."

"Spill it," said Rebecca.

"It's just that there's some pretty bad conflict between us lately—between the members of The Vision. And I'm afraid it's going to mess up our performance."

"What's going on?" asked Rebecca.

Penny looked over her sister's shoulder into the distance. "I'm hoping you two—investigative reporters that you are—can help me get to the bottom of that and fix the problem. Here comes Rachel now."

"Rachel?"

"The drummer. I invited her to come for dessert and talk about it. Is that okay?"

Rebecca and I looked at each other.

"Absolutely," I said.

"We'll be glad to listen," said Rebecca.

A moment later, Rachel—who looked like the embodiment of summer with her streaky blond hair and glowing tan—had been introduced to Rebecca and me and had taken her seat. Rebecca ordered the whoopie pie sampler for dessert, and soon, the waiter brought out a large tray with small cream-filled pies in every imaginable flavor.

"Now, tell us what's going on with your band," said Rebecca, biting into a red velvet pie.

"Well, the thing is, I'm dating Ken—our guitarist," said Rachel. "I know, I know." She held up both hands, one of which had a key lime whoopie pie in it. "I broke the cardinal rule in dating a member of the band. I couldn't help myself."

"So, you're in love?" asked Rebecca, resting her chin in her hand.

"Very much so," said Rachel. "We've only been together for a month. We fell for each other when we travelled together to North Carolina, for Songs of the

South. But frankly, I could see myself spending the rest of my life with Ken."

"That's wonderful, isn't it?" I asked, confused as to what the problem was.

"It would be if it weren't for Hayley," said Rachel.

"Your keyboard player?"

"That's right. She, well . . ."

"She dated Ken too," Penny finished.

"For like three years," said Rachel.

"So, you broke two cardinal rules," I said. "You dated a member of your own band *and* dated your friend's ex."

"Yep," said Rachel. "I feel awful about it. But it just happened, you know? And I didn't steal him from her or anything like that. Hayley and Ken had been broken up for a good while before he asked me out." She grinned at the memory. "He was so sweet. I couldn't resist. But now I'm torn between the joy and the guilt." She looked at Penny. "There's a song in there somewhere. We should work on that."

Penny nodded in agreement. "Absolutely."

"Anyway, Hayley and I aren't getting along, and it's definitely affecting our music in the worst way. We just don't jive anymore. I don't want to break up the band, but I also don't want to break up with the man I love—or break my own heart." She looked at Penny again. "That's catchy. Am I right?"

"*Definitely* a song in that," said Penny.

"I don't know what to do," said Rachel with a groan. She looked out toward the water and brightened. "Look! There's Ken now. He said he was going for a swim, and I told him I was coming here." She waved her whoopie pie in the direction of what had to be her perfect match, physically at least. Tall and muscular, longish blond hair, intense eyes, just the right amount of beard—Ken was the epitome of the surfer dude. He was still wet from his swim but had pulled on a t-shirt.

He walked up to our table and took Rachel's free hand. "Couldn't stay away," he said, smiling at her with perfectly straight, white teeth.

Rebecca and I looked at each other.

"Where have I seen him before?" I whispered to her.

"In the photo of The Vision?"

"Yes, but somewhere else, too . . . He's so familiar."

"Oh—I bet you saw the photos of the Bryant family when you checked in at Hideaway House. On the bookshelves when you first come in?"

That was it. I'd been perusing the lending library when I'd noticed what a beautiful family they were. When Jane had seen me admiring the photos, she'd told me they were of the owner's family. There were some snapshots of Ken, who was chatting quietly with Rachel now, and some of a beautiful little girl. There were a few where one parent or the other was in the photo, or where the children were smiling together—usually doing something like holding up a fish they'd just caught or proudly showing off a sandcastle or waving from the deck of a very nice sailboat. I liked it that there was no formal family portrait. Only these casual snapshots. It felt as if we really were in someone's comfortable living room. And the photos formed a lovely homage to the many summers the family had enjoyed on Purple Finch Island. The kids had been lucky enough to grow up returning again and again to this magical place.

"Ken, this is Eloise Lewis. She's our cousin from Vermont," said Penny.

"Nice to meet you, Eloise," Ken said, giving me a friendly smile and a handshake.

"So, your family owns Hideaway House?" I asked, picking out a chocolate cream whoopie pie. "It's such a gorgeous place."

"Thanks," Ken said with a smile. "We love it too. It's a really important part of my childhood—almost like an old friend to me."

"Eloise can relate," said Rebecca. "Her family owns an inn too. In Williamsbridge."

"Cool! I'm pretty sure I drove through there a few years back. Beautiful little town. Love to hike the Green Mountains," said Ken. "So did all of you grow up visiting Vermont, hanging out together?" He waved a hand at Rebecca, Penny, and me.

I shook my head. "This is the first time we've actually met in person. It's a long story."

"Basically, some of our family members from way back didn't get along," added Rebecca. "The family split up. But now we're pulling it back together."

Ken nodded. "Oh, I get that. Family relationship are complicated. Like, my sister and I love Hideaway House. But my brother wants nothing to do with it. He's hardly ever here. But Julie and I—we'd live here year-round if the winters weren't so harsh."

"I'm with you," said Rachel, beaming at Ken.

I wondered whether that was why Ken's brother wasn't in any of the family photos back at the inn. He didn't like it here. I looked out at the pink sky, doubled by its reflection on the water, and was astonished that it could be possible not to love such a paradise.

After a little more small talk, the two lovebirds stood to go. Before she left, Rachel invited us to join her for her usual early morning swim at the inn's pool, but all three of us declined. We were planning to sleep as late as we wanted—no early mornings for us.

"Then I guess we'll see you later," Rachel said, and she and Ken wandered off hand-in-hand to take a walk down the beach.

"There's no way those two are going to split up," said Penny, shaking her head as she watched them go. "In too deep to see that their relationship might cost the band its big chance."

"How long did Hayley date Ken?" I asked.

"Three years," said Penny. "They even lived together for a while. It was pretty serious."

"And who broke it off?" asked Rebecca.

"He did. He said Hayley was just too dramatic—and that their relationship had run its course. They still seemed to be on friendly terms, so I was hoping The Vision would weather the storm. But then Ken and Rachel paired up, and now I'm not so sure. What should I do?"

"Good question," Rebecca said. "Maybe talk to Hayley."

"Maybe there's a way to have some sort of intervention—to get the three of them to talk it out and decide whether the band is going to stay a priority, and whether they can put this aside," I suggested.

"Like an intervention . . ." Penny mused. "That might just work."

"Confrontations are sort of horrifying, though. Let's think some more about it," Rebecca said. "There's got to be a way to smooth the waters."

"Whatever we do, it's got to be fast," said Penny. "Because tomorrow night's the festival, and our performance will make or break The Vision."

CHAPTER 6

My eyes popped open early Saturday morning, even though Rebecca, Penny, and I had agreed we'd all sleep in. I was wide awake, excited to start a new day in paradise. And my mind was buzzing over Penny's problem with her band. Then it dawned on me. I was an advice columnist, for Pete's sake! I was actually *paid* to help people with problems like this one. What would Miss Smithers tell the girls in the band to do to make their music sweet again?

I glanced at the clock, then jumped out of bed, put on my swimsuit, pulled on a pair of shorts, and grabbed my beach bag before heading down to the pool. If I hurried, I could still catch Rachel, who should have been out for her morning swim right about then. Sure enough, she was there, swimming laps, slicing through the water like a knife. I dropped my bag at a table and went and sat with my feet in the cool water. When Rachel stopped for a breather, she spotted me and waved.

"Hey! I thought you were all hitting the snooze button this morning." She swam over and popped out of the pool, jogged to a nearby table and grabbed a towel, then returned and sat beside me. "How's it going? Are you all settled in?"

"Too settled in," I said with a laugh. "I could stay all summer!"

"Yep, this place has that effect." She looked across the pool to the lush blooms in the gardens and the deep blue ocean beyond and smiled. "It casts a spell."

"If you marry Ken, maybe you'll live here with him in the summers." I pointed at the small cottage that lay across the pool. "Is that his family's house?"

She nodded and sighed deeply. "Wouldn't that be amazing? I'm so excited about our life together."

"It's really cool that you both play in the band," I said, looking for a graceful segue. "But I was sorry to hear your music has been off lately because of the conflict with Hayley."

Rachel looked down into the water. "We used to be such good friends," she said quietly. "And she was happy with Ken for a long time. And I was happy for her. We all were. But she can't find it in her heart to be happy for me."

"Maybe you can talk it out with her," I said, channeling my inner Miss Smithers. "Make amends. Maybe if she understands how much you value her friendship—"

"Eloise, I've tried that already. She won't listen."

"If the situation were reversed—if you were watching her and Ken fall in love after he'd broken it off with you—"

"Eloise, don't even *think* that!" She tossed her towel away. "If Hayley wants to talk to me, great. If she wants to reach out and make amends, fine. But if she can't handle the fact that Ken and I are happy and in love, too bad. There comes a point where you have to take care of yourself and prioritize your own happiness!" She jumped back into the pool and swam away.

Defeated, I went back to the table where I'd left my beach bag. I took out a thick book and settled down to read. I was actually glad when my phone rang, because I was having a heck of a time concentrating on the words. I smiled when I looked at the screen. It was Matthew. Probably calling to tell me he missed me.

"Hi," I said, smiling into the receiver.

"Hi El. Listen, where do we keep that old metal cookie tin? The one your mom uses for pecan candy every Thanksgiving?"

"I, uh, in the cabinets above the refrigerator. Why?"

"Carol and Stacey want to use it as a prop."

"How's the murder mystery weekend going?"

"Great! We got a really fun group of participants. They're having a heck of a time solving this one."

"Oh. Good." I really was glad. But I also felt another emotion . . . something akin to disappointment—but not. Why should it bother me that Matthew and the Blake sisters could pull off an event without me? Or that Matthew had called for a practical purpose rather than a romantic one?

"El? You okay? How's island life?"

"What? Oh, it's amazing. You should see this place."

"I should," he agreed.

My smile came back at the warmth in his voice. "Call me tonight?"

"Will do."

As soon as I hung up, I decided that since my advice to Rachel hadn't taken hold, maybe I should call Edna and get some insight from her. After all, she'd been Miss Smithers before me—and had given out sound advice for almost fifteen years. I eyed Rachel, who was still gliding through the water. *How many laps did she swim every day?* Then again, that explained why she looked so great. I tucked my book into my bag and followed a winding path through the garden and all the way out to the beach, where only a few early risers were out, either jogging or fishing. I took my phone out and called Edna.

"Well good morning, stranger," she said cheerily from the other end of the line.

"I knew you'd be up early," I said. "What's on the menu today?"

"Vermont Cheddar, Creamy Tomato-Basil Bisque, and Felix and I are experimenting with a cold Borscht, for summer."

"Beets, right?"

"Yep. And sour cream and potatoes and onion and cucumber . . . we're serving it with hard boiled eggs and crusty bread."

"Sounds amazing."

"What are you doing up so early? Aren't you supposed to be on vacation?"

"Old habits die hard. Hey, can I get your advice about something?"

"Of course! Is everything okay?"

"Oh, I'm fine. This advice is for someone else." I told Edna all about The Vision, and the love triangle within it.

"It's almost never a good idea to date a person you work with—you and Matthew excepted, of course."

"Much less date your friend's ex," I said.

"And Rachel isn't willing to try to talk to Hayley again?"

"She says she's done, that Hayley will have to reach out to her."

"Then I'd say your best bet is to talk to Hayley. Get her side of the story. There are almost certainly details Rachel's left out. Maybe talking to Hayley will help you understand the full situation, and then you can offer better advice."

"Good idea," I said. "Thanks Edna."

"Anytime, Eloise. We miss you. Oh—and thanks for sending me a photo of that delectable-looking soup you had last night. I'll have to work out the recipe when you get home."

Edna and I hung up, and I resolved to somehow talk to Hayley if the opportunity ever presented itself. Of course, I could ask Penny to introduce us, and maybe then Penny could help me broach the conversation with Hayley. After all, Penny had asked Rebecca and me to help. My thoughts were interrupted by raised voices coming from a couple who were walking along the beach, headed in my direction. Their voices were getting louder by the second, so I decided to make myself scarce before they got any nearer. People really should go inside to have their heated arguments. I glanced at the couple before turning away and realized I'd seen both of them before.

One was Hayley. I recognized her striking red hair from the photo Penny had shown me of The Vision. The other, with his tousled blond hair, bronzed skin, and "Hang Ten" tank top, was Ken. Hayley and Ken, together on the beach? I instinctively strained to hear what they were saying, but the steady pounding of the surf and the chatter of the sea birds made it impossible to understand anything but their angry tone.

Clearly, this was not the time to meet Hayley—much less come up with a way to encourage her to forgive Rachel and put the fate of the band ahead of her feelings about Ken and Rachel's budding romance. By the heat in their argument, it would appear there was still some unfinished business between Hayley and Ken. I turned and hurried back to the inn.

CHAPTER 7

By the time I returned to my room, Rebecca and Penny were up and had ordered a lavish breakfast from room service, which was being set up on our shared balcony. I tossed my beach bag on the bed and opened the glass door wide to let the sea breezes into my room. Breakfast was delicious. There were huge, puffed pancakes, covered in berries, and drizzled with maple syrup, and baked eggs with vegetables and goat cheese.

"I love these puffed pancakes," said Rebecca. "I eat them here every year, and always wish I could find a place that serves them at home."

"We make them at the inn for our guests," I said. "They're easy."

Penny looked at her plate. "You're kidding."

"Seriously. They're simple to make. I'll give you the recipe so you can have them anytime you want."

"Great!" said Rebecca.

We finished eating, coated ourselves in sunscreen, and headed out to the beach. We walked until we found a nice open space and set ourselves up under one of the umbrellas the inn provided for its guests. Rebecca and I took out our stacks of books while Penny ran off into the surf. I kept my eyes open for Hayley, but never saw her again. A few hours later, the soft breeze, the lapping of the waves, and the warmth of the sun had put me to sleep. Rebecca had apparently succumbed to the relaxing atmosphere as well because we both woke with a start when Penny ran up and dripped cool water onto us as she reached for a towel.

"You two were clearly cut from the same cloth," she said with a laugh.

I yawned and stretched. "Rachel told me this place casts a spell, and she was right. I can't remember the last time I felt this relaxed."

"Isn't it wonderful?" said Rebecca.

"I've got to get to practice with the band," said Penny. "Hopefully Rachel and Hayley will be able to tolerate each other. If not, we need to talk more about that intervention idea this afternoon, okay?"

"Of course," I said. "Just let us know."

"Will do," said Penny, then she wrapped herself in her towel and headed back to the inn.

"How would you like to get a little preview of tonight's show?" Rebecca asked, taking her tablet computer from her bag.

"That'd be great," I said, scooting my beach chair closer to hers.

Rebecca pulled up a video of one of The Vision's biggest hits, "When You Think About Me." In the video, each of the girls was shown in a different scenario. Penny was depicted as a young woman leaving home for the first time. Rachel was a woman leaving an unfulfilling job to pursue a dream. Hayley was leaving a bad relationship, and Ken played the guy she was walking away from. The song relayed a positive message of empowerment and self-confidence.

"Wow. They're amazing," I said when the video ended. "They're as good as a lot of the bands you hear on the radio. They could really make it big."

"Yep," said Rebecca. "If they can sort out their problems and learn to get along again."

That night, the grassy lawns of the inn and the beach that ran in front of it were covered with blankets and folding chairs as the music festival got underway. Rebecca and I brought along a big blanket and one of the inn's take-along baskets, which was filled with fruit, cheese, crackers, and a bottle of sweet wine.

A large stage had been set up in a big open area on the lawn and was banked by a couple of huge screens that would be streaming the stage happenings so that people seated further away could see. The host for the evening came out and announced that the opening band was getting ready to come onstage, and then proceeded to regale the audience with jokes. Everyone was soon in great spirits and revved up for the music.

Vendors occasionally walked by, selling fun glowing headbands and bracelets, souvenir fans and programs, and interesting snacks and drinks, like waffles on sticks dipped in chocolate or drinks served in coconut shells with colorful twisty straws and tiny umbrellas.

"I can't even remember the last time I went to a concert," I said, handing some bills over to a young man in exchange for a program with photos and descriptions of the bands.

"I'm so nervous for Penny," Rebecca said, taking a sip of wine. "I can't imagine actually *wanting* to get up on stage and perform. I'll stick to writing, thank you very much."

"I'm with you," I said. "I wouldn't want to be famous, either. I'd much rather live in my little hometown and run my inn." I looked around. "I really hope your sister had a chance to talk to the rest of the group. They're too talented to let anything get in their way."

"She never called to talk about it this afternoon, so they must've gotten their act together."

The first band—a group called Tree People—came onstage, and sang their original hit, "We Will Redeem

You." Close on their heels was Froggy Pop, with "Little Dream." Then we heard Sara's Band play their song, "Miss You."

Listening to that song took my thoughts to Matthew. I wondered what he was doing . . . wondered if he was missing me. I suddenly wished he was there with me, in that magical moment, sitting on that blanket under the stars, sipping wine and listening to that love song. I loved Purple Finch Island. But my heart was in Williamsbridge, Vermont.

CHAPTER 8

Rebecca began to fidget as the seventh band on the program wrapped up their performance. Down Cellar had presented their catchy, original song, "Chuppta," to a rousing round of applause.

"Wow," I said as they exited the stage with the audience yelling for an encore, "they're really popular."

"They're a big deal around here. Tough act to follow," Rebecca said. Then she began to fidget again, drumming her fingers nervously on the side of her wineglass.

"I don't even know what that song meant," I said, hoping to distract Rebecca. "*Chuppta*? What's that?"

She laughed. "That's Maine-speak for *What are you up to*. Get it? Chuppta."

"I get it now! Funny."

"What's taking them so long?"

"Who?"

"The Vision. They should be coming out onstage. Where's that host? The guy with all the jokes . . ." She looked around.

"I'm sure they'll be out in a minute," I said, although as the minutes stretched out, it did seem odd that there was a longer break than there had been between bands up until then. "Look, there's host-guy."

Sure enough, our host for the evening made his way out onto the stage and took the mike. "Everyone feel free to take a moment to get yourself a snack or souvenir. Our next band will be out in a jiff."

"Something's wrong. I can feel it," said Rebecca, setting down her wine glass and standing to look around.

"Do you want to go check on Penny?" I asked. "Although with this crowd, it'll be hard to get backstage."

Rebecca hesitated. "I guess I could try texting her. But I doubt—"

Just then a bone-chilling scream rang out. It sounded like it had come from backstage.

"Oh no. I knew it!" Rebecca began weaving through the people around us toward the stage. All heads turned in the direction of the scream, and after a beat of silence, a curious mumbling arose from the crowd.

Host-guy was still onstage at the mike, but in mid-sentence, he looked to his right, spotted something behind the curtain, and went quiet—and pale. He almost dropped the microphone as his arm went limp at his side, but then he managed to put it back into its caddy with trembling hands.

By that time, Rebecca and I had politely said "excuse me" about a hundred times as we stepped over and around people. We found a festival volunteer, and Rebecca said, "My sister's in the next band. Something's wrong. I need to get backstage." The volunteer waved over a member of the crew, who nodded and took us back. What we saw upon rounding the corner shocked us to the core. There, at the edge of the curtain, stood Hayley, a group of people around her—and there was blood all over her white t-shirt. She was clearly upset, so we moved in closer as quickly as possible.

"I'm telling you, we can't find her anywhere. Can you just go on with the next act and work us in later?"

Rebecca and I both spotted Penny at the same moment and rushed over to her.

"What's happening?" Rebecca asked, hugging her younger sister, and then looking her over to make sure she was all in one piece. "I had the worst feeling a moment ago that something is terribly wrong."

"Something *is* wrong," said Penny.

"Was that you who screamed?"

"No, it was one of the backstage attendants. She'd just seen Hayley over there, with blood on her shirt. I think she was just startled."

"Understandable," I said. "Is Hayley hurt?"

"She doesn't seem to be," said Penny. "I haven't been able to get to her to ask."

"What's with the blood then?" asked Rebecca.

"I don't know, but right now, all I care about is finding Rachel. We're going to blow our big chance. The scout from Maine Tunes Records is out there in the audience—did you see him? Already we look like an undependable group, since we just threw off the whole festival schedule. This isn't going to sit well at all."

"Let's go look for Rachel," Rebecca said.

We heard host-guy out on the stage again. He'd recovered his composure and was announcing the next band, apologizing to the crowd for the delay. We heard him say, "The Vision must've had *a vision* that they'd be late!"

The audience laughed.

"Oh great," said Penny. "We're finished!"

"Let's go find Rachel. When they hear you, they'll forget all about this," said Rebecca.

After looking in the backstage dressing rooms, we went back over to the inn, thinking perhaps Rachel was in her room. Maybe she'd gotten sick or fallen asleep or lost track of the time.

"She sometimes gets into writing a song and sort of loses herself," said Penny as we hurried along, Hayley and Ken just a few steps behind us. "She writes a lot of our lyrics, and Hayley writes the music," Penny explained. "Creative types can be hard to pin down, you know?"

Rebecca and I looked at each other and shrugged simultaneously. We were both writers, but our creativity came in the form of putting what we saw in the world into words. If Matthew, with his fantasy novels, painted pictures with words, I took photographs with words. The best journalists strive to depict what they see so accurately that the reader is almost standing there next to them, seeing it too.

When we came to Rachel's second-floor room, which was called *Mermaid Lagoon*, we knocked. When she didn't answer, we tried the knob. When we found the door to be locked, we turned to Ken.

"Do you have a key?" Penny asked, holding out her hand. "I remember Rachel gave you a key."

Ken patted his pockets. "I changed down at the festival," he said. "My key is backstage. I'll go get the manager." He disappeared down the hall and we continued to knock, text, call, pound, yell . . . trying everything we could think of to bring Rachel out into the hallway, to no avail.

A few minutes later, Ken came jogging down the hall again with Jane Gander.

"It's this one," Ken said.

"Of course, Mr. Bryant," said Jane, slipping her master key into the lock and opening the door.

Inside, all the lights were on, as was the television. A cute outfit—a miniskirt, t-shirt, and a pair of beaded flip flops was laid out on the bed, along with a pair of drumsticks. Several other sets of sticks and an electronic drum set, presumably for practicing, covered the desk. Magazines and sneakers and articles of clothing littered the room. It looked lived-in, as if Rachel had just been there a moment before. I looked at the closed bathroom door and noticed light shining out from under it.

"She might be in there," I said, pointing.

Penny hurried over and knocked urgently. When there was no answer, she threw open the door.

And screamed.

CHAPTER 9

"Looks like electrocution," I heard a police detective say under his breath to the officer he was conferring with. "She was probably in a hurry to get over to the festival and decided to blow-dry her hair while she was taking a bath. If I've seen it once, I've seen it a thousand times."

"You've seen this before?"

"Nope."

The detective—a man who, based on his appearance, struck me as more Magnum P.I. than Columbo—had introduced himself to us as Bill Redding, "But you can call me Bill." His straitlaced sidekick was Officer Babbish. ("You can call me Officer Babbish.") We were told to stand by, that they would secure the scene and take our statements as soon as possible, so we stood leaning against a wall in the hallway just outside the door to Rachel's room.

I leaned over to Rebecca. "If a detective is here, do you think that means . . ."

Rebecca nodded, quickly understanding. "I think they need to be sure nothing fishy is going on. It's probably just a formality. At least I hope so."

"I requested that the detective come along," said Jane, who stood in the hallway with us. "I want no stone left unturned."

"Ms. Gander, can you come here please?" the detective called from inside the room.

Jane went inside and I tried to hear what they were saying.

"They're asking Jane about the security cameras in the hallways," whispered Rebecca.

"Too bad they're on the blink," said Ken.

We all turned to him.

"They are?" Penny asked.

"Yep. They have been for a while."

Jane returned to the hall, frowning. "Mr. Bryant, we really must address the security system immediately."

Ken nodded. "That's pretty obvious at this point," he said miserably.

I peered back into the room, where Bill and Officer Babbish were currently checking under the bed. "Do you think either of those guys has any experience with murder investigation?" I asked, thinking of our tiny police force back home, featuring the well-meaning but bumbling Detective Dunlap and Officer Potts.

"Kasko is a tiny village, and those two along with about two other officers are the whole police department here," said Jane. "We wouldn't even have that if it weren't for the tourists. Crime on Purple Finch Island basically amounts to pickpocketing, driving under the influence, and the occasional noise disturbance. A young person's very untimely death . . . right here at the inn . . ." She shook her head. "This is new territory."

Rebecca frowned as Officer Babbish tripped over the chord to Rachel's electronic drum set. "But I mean, if this turned out *not* to be a simple accident . . . they could handle it, right?"

"Like everyone else, they move over to the mainland during the winter. But there's not much crime over at Sea Star Bay either." Jane sighed, then brightened a little. "They caught the kid who was stealing the hermit crabs from Catch of the Day last week."

"Stealing hermit crabs?"

"Turned out he was taking them out to the coast and setting them free," said Jane. "The owners didn't press charges. In fact, they ended up hiring the kid to oversee hermit crab care at the shop after that."

"Happy ending," Rebecca said, a sad note in her voice. "Not like this." She looked back into the room.

I strained to hear what Bill and Officer Babbish were saying. They kept mentioning electrocution but avoiding even going into the bathroom. A moment later, the EMTs arrived, and Bill got on the phone with the coroner.

"No one blow-dries their hair in the bathtub," Penny whispered as we all watched. "Rachel was too smart for that."

Ken, who hadn't said a word, just nodded, glassy-eyed.

"Besides, all of the bathroom plugs in this inn are up to code," said Jane. "Every bathroom is fitted with GFCI outlets—and our hairdryers are new and up to code as well. I don't think it's even possible that that poor girl would've been electrocuted, even if she did try to dry her hair while taking a bath."

"Be sure to tell Detective, er, Bill that when he takes your statement," said Rebecca.

"Oh, I will." Jane sighed. "I just hope that if Rachel was, well," she lowered her voice to a whisper, "*murdered*, that they find the killer immediately."

All heads turned back to Bill and Babbish, and a palpable cloud of doubt settled over us.

"We have to find out what happened to Rachel," said Penny. She looked at Ken. "Because if someone hurt her, they're going to pay for it."

"What are you looking at me for?" Ken said. "I'd never hurt Rachel."

"The door was locked when we got here, Ken. If someone went in there and killed her and then locked it back . . . Who else but you had a key?"

"I don't know, but it's not cool that you could even *think*—"

"I'll think whatever I want to think. You know good and well—"

"Shove it, Penny!"

"Now, hold on," I said. "Before this gets any further out of hand, let's stop and think about this. The police are going to do a full investigation—"

"Those two?" said Penny. "Seriously?"

"Well, maybe we can help them out a little."

Rebecca turned to me. "Help them out how?"

"By doing a little investigating of our own," I whispered.

"Us?" Rebecca looked at me in disbelief.

Penny stepped forward. "Can we? How?"

"I have a little bit of experience with this," I said. And it was true. Matthew and I had helped our own

Dunlap and Potts solve more than one mystery back home in Williamsbridge.

"You do?" Rebecca raised a brow.

"Well—yes. I know it sounds odd. But Matthew and I—"

"That cute guy you date?" asked Penny.

I nodded. "We've solved this kind of thing before." I looked at Rebecca. "We're reporters. We're natural investigators."

"I don't know about that." Rebecca looked at me doubtfully. "I usually keep a safe distance from the things I write about."

"Trust me. You know more than you think you do and you're braver than you think you are." I looked back into the room as the EMTs emerged from the bathroom with a covered body on a stretcher. I thought of Rachel, swimming laps that morning, talking about love and her future, so full of joy, so alive . . . "We can help make sure the killer doesn't get away with this."

"Good," said Jane. "You let me know if you need help. I'm at your service."

A few minutes later, Bill and Babbish split us up and took our statements. There wasn't much to say, really, so it didn't take long. We were told they would call us again if they had further questions, and then released. Rebecca, Penny, and I trudged up the stairs and into our rooms. We all went out onto the balcony and sat down, feeling exhausted.

"There's no way I'm sleeping tonight," said Penny.

"Me neither," said Rebecca with a shiver.

"Let's order coffee," said Penny.

"Great idea." I got up. "I'm going to change into sweats."

"I'll order pie, too," said Rebecca. "They have an amazing strawberry pie here. We can talk about our investigation."

"Perfect," I said, and ducked into my room. I opened a drawer, took out my comfiest sweats and t-shirt, and got changed, washed my face, and pulled my hair into a bun. Then I decided to give Matthew a quick call to get his perspective on the situation.

"How terrible," he said after I'd filled him in.

"I want to do a little investigating, but—"

"Of course, you do."

"*But* I don't know where to start. I need to figure out what the first step would be. The first possible suspect that comes to mind is the boyfriend, Ken, of course," I said. "He had a key to the room. He was closest to the victim."

"On the other hand, everyone knows the boyfriend would be the first suspect. Maybe the killer was counting on that. Maybe they were hoping it would get pinned on this Ken guy. I mean, how stupid would Ken have to be to kill his girlfriend in her room when no one else had a key?" I could tell Matthew was shaking his head across the miles. "No, I think if he'd killed her, he would've done it somewhere else."

"Well, then that leaves Hayley."

"The keyboard player?" asked Matthew.

"Right. She used to date Ken and was furious that he and Rachel were together. It was actually ruining things for the band—the conflict between the two women."

"A crime of passion."

"Oh—I'd almost forgotten! I saw Hayley and Ken together on the beach this morning."

"Really? That wouldn't have sat well with his new girlfriend. What were they doing on the beach?"

"Arguing."

"About . . ."

"I couldn't hear."

"Well, then there's your first step. Find out what Hayley and Ken were arguing about. Take Rebecca with you. She's a reporter, like you. Between the two of you, you can listen and notice body language. And since neither of you is in the band, you'll be the most objective."

I smiled. "That's exactly what I'll do. Thank you."

"You're welcome."

"Hey—how's the murder mystery going?"

"Great! In fact, the Blake sisters asked if we'd be interested in doing more of these weekends. They want to help out. They were even saying they thought we could host an event a couple times a month during the off-season. What do you think?"

"I love it!" I felt giddy with excitement. Murder mystery weekends at the inn were a blast, and the perfect solution to staying busy year-round. "We can run it by Mom when I get home, but I think that sounds great."

"Good."

I heard the doorbell in the next room ding and knew the coffee and pie had arrived. "I'd better go. Rebecca and Penny are waiting."

"Okay." He paused. "Please be careful, El. Okay?"

"I will."

Another pause. "I miss you."

I smiled. "I miss you too. I love—" The three little words had almost come rolling right out, as natural as if I'd been talking about the weather, or what I'd had for dinner.

"You love . . ."

"Oh, to heck with it," I said, feeling a wave of courage. "I love you. Sorry I'm saying that for the first time when we're hundreds of miles apart. I should have—"

"I love you too."

"You do?"

"Of course."

"Okay then." I felt a bubbling joy rising in my throat, threatening to come out as laughter. "Good."

"I'm smiling so big my face hurts," Matthew said.

"Me too."

"Talk to you tomorrow. Be safe."

"I will."

I went back out to the balcony, knowing that it was more than Rachel's death that would be keeping me awake that night.

CHAPTER 10

On Sunday morning, Rebecca and I had our early-morning coffee out on our balcony while Penny slept in.

"She had a rough night," Rebecca said, closing the door softly behind her and pouring herself a mug from the carafe. "Rachel was one of her closest friends. This is just awful."

"It might help bring closure if we can make sure whoever killed Rachel is brought to justice," I said.

"I know we talked about this last night . . . But we're sure it wasn't just an accident, right? I mean, we're absolutely sure she wasn't electrocuted in her bathtub?"

"We won't know that positively until after the coroner's report comes in. But Jane doesn't think that's what happened."

Rebecca nodded and swallowed. "I've always felt that I'm not brave enough—that I tend to stay on the sidelines, where it's safe. But I want to help solve this thing, whatever that means." She looked at me. "So where do we begin?"

The night before, Rebecca and I had ended up spending more time comforting Penny and listening to her stories about Rachel than planning our investigation. It was for the best. Penny needed to grieve, and we needed a clearer picture of the kind of person Rachel had been.

"We need to talk to Ken and try to find out what he and Hayley were arguing about on the beach."

Rebecca yawned, then took another sip of hot coffee. "Hopefully he'll be receptive to that conversation."

After a little more caffeine therapy, the two of us quietly left to search for Ken.

"I know Ken's family owns this inn and they have their own cottage on the grounds. Do you think that's where Ken is staying?"

"I imagine so," said Rebecca. "I think I remember Penny mentioning it."

We emerged from our building into the lush gardens that surrounded the pool. The quaint cottage sat on the opposite side, down a little cobbled path through flower beds brimming with hydrangeas and beach roses. We didn't even need to approach the cottage, though, because Ken was sitting alone by the pool, staring out at the water. We sat quietly down beside him.

"She came here early every morning," he said, his eyes never leaving the water. "Never missed her morning swim. She asked me to go with her, but I always had some excuse."

"I saw her out here yesterday morning," I said. "She was quite an accomplished swimmer."

Ken nodded. "She was." His eyes filled with tears. "She asked me to swim with her yesterday, but I . . ." He shook his head.

"Why didn't you?" Rebecca asked gently.

"I, uh, I'd been up late the night before. I slept in." He put his head in his hands and I caught Rebecca's eyes.

"That's funny. I'm sure I saw you out on the beach early yesterday morning."

Ken frowned at me. "What? No, I don't know what you're talking about."

"You were arguing with Hayley. Right out there, just down from the inn." I pointed in the direction of the beach.

"No, I wasn't. I don't remember anything like that." He ran tan fingers through his blond hair.

Clearly, Ken was either lying or had a very bad memory, and I knew I'd risk losing him altogether if I kept insisting. I decided to try another tack. "Ken, can you think of anyone who would want to harm Rachel?"

Ken let out a long, exasperated sigh. "Everyone loved Rachel, except—" He looked at Rebecca and me, a guilty expression on his face. "Well, lately, Hayley hadn't been getting along with her."

"Hadn't been getting along . . . because of your relationship with Rachel?"

Ken nodded, then looked at his sports watch. "Oh, man, I've gotta go. That Detective Bill called me in for more questions." Ken leaned closer to Rebecca and me, folding his hands on the table. "Thing is, they think *I* did it. Everyone thinks I did it. I was closest to Rachel, I was the last person known to have seen her, I had a key to the room . . ." He looked around and lowered his voice. "But it's got to be Hayley who did it. Right? No one else had any beef with Rachel. She was—" His voice caught in his throat. "She was the kindest, best, most beautiful spirit." He frowned. "But you know what's crazy? I thought Hayley and Rachel had finally made up." He started to stand, but I grabbed his arm.

"Hold on. What do you mean, they'd made up?"

Ken settled back into his seat. "Last night, before the festival, we all had dinner together—the three of us. I was trying to get them to work things out, and they did. I mean, I thought so, anyway. It wasn't easy. There was some serious tension for sure. But we all knew that scout from Maine Tunes was going to be in the audience last night, and we agreed that the band was our top priority. We wanted our big shot, you know? Hayley and Rachel talked it out and finally agreed to let bygones be bygones." He shook his head. "We all decided to rest up before the concert. I went with Rachel to her room. Fell sound asleep, and next think I knew, we were only an hour away from the festival opening. I headed over to the dressing room at the stage, and Rachel said she was going to take a bath, have a cup of hot tea, and get changed in the room. I offered to bring her the tea but ended up ordering room service instead. We were short on time. Speaking of—" He tapped his watch. "Ah, man, I have to go." He stood and trudged off toward the parking lot.

Rebecca fell back in her chair. "So, the killer might be Hayley."

"Or Ken," I said.

"I'm ordering breakfast here by the pool," said Rebecca, picking up a menu from the table. "We need to rehash everything Ken just said."

"Two things are bothering me," I said. "Why was Hayley's shirt covered with blood last night? And why did Ken lie about arguing with her?"

CHAPTER 11

Rebecca and I discussed what we knew so far—which wasn't much—over fried eggs with toast and bacon.

"Ken seemed really and truly heartbroken," said Rebecca, sipping her second cup of coffee.

"But then why lie about his argument with Hayley?" I spread honey on a slice of toast. Rebecca and I had talked ourselves in circles and were now returning to the beginning of our conversation—and we were no closer to knowing what to do next. "The thing to do now is to talk to Hayley."

Rebecca gasped and leaned close to me. "That might be difficult . . ." she whispered, nodding in the direction of the door that led from our wing of the inn out into the gardens.

There was Hayley, in handcuffs, being led by Officer Babbish out of the building and up the garden path toward the parking area. Detective Bill, who had changed to a different but equally loud tropical shirt, was beside him and Penny was right behind them. When she saw Rebecca and me, she put a hand on Hayley's shoulder and the two exchanged a nod. Hayley looked pale and frightened—understandably.

Penny came over and sat down at our table. "This just gets worse and worse," she said, pouring herself a cup of coffee and adding cream and sugar. "Hayley is horrified. The grief of losing Rachel coupled with being arrested? This is going to do her in!"

"Did the detective find some new evidence or something?" I asked. "Because those handcuffs indicate Hayley isn't just going in for more questioning."

"I was there when they arrested her," said Penny. "I had just walked down to Hayley's room to check on her, but the police were already there. They said the forensics report came back, and you know that blood that was all over Hayley's shirt? It was Rachel's."

"Oh no," said Rebecca. "Do you think it's possible that Hayley killed her? We were just talking to Ken, and he—"

"But Rachel was electrocuted, right?" Penny interrupted her sister. "I mean, there wasn't any blood, was there?"

Rebecca and I were silent for a moment.

"I didn't get a good look," I said, wishing I could wipe away the sight of Rachel's pale arm hanging over the side of the bathtub from my memory. "But I'm sure that's what Detective Bill thought last night."

"Maybe the fact that Rachel's blood was on Hayley's shirt is enough to cast suspicion, though," said Penny. "Even if there was no blood at the actual scene."

"That makes sense," said Rebecca. She looked at Penny. "Does it seem possible that Hayley and Rachel got into a fight? I mean, like a physical fight?"

Penny shook her head. "I just can't imagine that. I could see them yelling at each other. Or being really cold to each other. But not actually having, like, a fistfight."

"Well, Rachel's blood got on Hayley's shirt somehow," I said.

"Oh, I've got it!" Penny said suddenly. "Why didn't I think of it sooner? Rachel got nosebleeds. She got them all the time. She even got them as a kid. She had terrible allergies. Maybe she got one yesterday before the festival and Hayley was with her." Penny thought for a moment. "But that doesn't make sense either, because they weren't speaking."

"Yes, they were," I said. "We just had a little chat with Ken. He said they had dinner last night before the concert. They made up."

"Seriously?" Penny fell back in her chair and put her hands on her head. "So, then we might've . . . They were willing to get onstage together. We could've done a good show. The scout would've seen, and who knows?" She shook her head. "And now we'll never play together again."

Rebecca put a hand on her sister's. "Don't give up that dream just yet, Penny. Maybe another door will open someday."

Penny looked at Rebecca, and tears filled her eyes. "I'm a jerk for even thinking about the band or the concert or the scout or any of it. Rachel's dead. One of my two dearest friends is gone forever, and the other is in jail." She stood. "I've got to go. I'm going down to the police station to check on Hayley. I need to make sure she's been able to get in touch with her parents and see if there's anything I can do for her." She looked from Rachel to me. "I know Hayley didn't kill Rachel. I know it's a lot to ask, but please, *please* try to find out who did."

Penny walked briskly down the path and disappeared under an arch of blooms.

"So, Rachel was supposedly electrocuted, but Hayley had blood on her shirt," said Rebecca. "We need to find out what happened after they had dinner together last night."

"And whether Rachel was electrocuted at all," I said.

CHAPTER 12

Rebecca and I had signed up for an oyster-shucking class at the Lobster Pot in the village at lunchtime on Sunday.

"Should we still go?" I asked, not sure whether it felt right to continue on with our vacation plans after all that had happened.

"I think we should," Rebecca said. "It might help us to take a break. Even have a little fun. We'll take our class, maybe do a little shopping . . . Who knows? Maybe we'll have a breakthrough."

"I can't tell you how wonderful that sounds," I said.

We got cleaned up and climbed into the little car Rebecca had rented and drove into the village.

"There's the Lobster Pot," said Rebecca, pointing to the restaurant that sat tucked into the wharf. There were tables scattered over a wide wooden dock where people sat, cracking into lobsters and watching the boats sail past. "You hop out and go tell them we're here. I'll find a parking spot and catch up with you."

I got out of the car and Rebecca sped away. As I walked toward the Lobster Pot, I looked into the windows of the quaint shops that lined Sea Lavender Lane. There were jars of colorful candy on offer in Taffy's Candy Shop and Fudge Kitchen. There were bowls brimming with beautiful shells in Sea Glass, and Purple Finch Island t-shirts hanging in the windows at Catch of the Day, along with bins of sunscreen, beach floats, cheap sunglasses, and even used romance novels for readers who, unlike Rebecca and me, *hadn't* brought too many books from home. Out on the dock, you could pay a man in a pirate costume five dollars to have your picture taken with a bright green parrot on your shoulder.

As I glanced across the street at the High Flyin' Kite Shop, a head of scruffy blond hair caught my eye. It was Ken, walking down the street. Ken, who had changed out of his usual surfer dude attire and was dressed smartly in a polo shirt and Bermuda shorts with loafers. He looked like he was headed to the club for a day of sailing or yachting or something . . . And he didn't look a bit sad or forlorn, like he had earlier.

I hesitated for a moment, but then decided to try to get his attention. "Ken!" I called.

He didn't hear me.

"Ken! Over here!"

No response. He just kept walking at the same brisk clip. I paused, not knowing what to do. Bottom line, I didn't know Ken well. We'd just met. And I was beginning to feel awkward as people looked at me, standing there calling out to a person who clearly either couldn't hear me or didn't want to.

Rebecca came jogging up just as I was deciding whether or not to follow Ken. I told her what had happened.

"Very strange behavior. We should trail him. See where he's going," she said.

I nodded and we hurried down the sidewalk in the direction Ken had gone. Just then, a tour bus pulled up next to us. The doors hissed as they opened, and a large group of sightseers trickled out, all of them wearing bright yellow shirts with the words *Gilmore Family Getaway* written across them. As they passed, we could see that each t-shirt featured the wearer's name on the back. "Aunt Peg" stepped right in front of us, along with "Uncle Rick" and "Grandpa Jeb."

"Oh, um, excuse us—" Rebecca started to say, just before "Aunt Dee" edged her out of the way.

"Sorry—we were just—" I tried getting around them, but the Gilmore family was, unfortunately, dominating the sidewalk.

Rebecca and I stopped walking, veered back around to the other side of the bus, and looked as far as we could see up the sidewalk, which branched off at every corner onto side streets that were all bustling.

"I think we lost him," I said, sighing.

Rebecca put an arm around me. "Let's just go to the Lobster Pot. We'll learn how to shuck oysters, eat some lunch, and regroup."

"Good idea," I said, and we turned and went back in the direction we'd come.

. . .

An hour and a half later, Rebecca and I had become oyster-shucking experts and had enjoyed a huge platter of fresh oysters, served on a bed of ice. We'd learned to pick up the half-shells and tip them into our mouths so that we could enjoy the liquor—like tasting a sample of the sea the oyster had come from. We had learned that a few drops of lemon juice and a dash of cocktail sauce were all that was needed, and that the tiny cocktail fork was meant to be used to loosen up the oyster meat—not pick it out of the shell. We had learned to make our own mignonette, a sauce of red wine vinegar, cracked black pepper, and scallions, for when we enjoyed shellfish at home, and we'd filled up on the Lobster Pot's amazing homemade bread and butter.

"Ugh, I need a nap," Rebecca said, patting her stomach as we walked down the street.

"You know, I've been thinking about seeing Ken earlier. I'm beginning to wonder if I was mistaken. I mean, how many blond-haired guys are here right now?"

Rebecca and I together scanned the sidewalks around us. There must've been fifteen bleach-blond men within our field of vision at that moment.

"Point taken," said Rebecca.

"And the guy I saw was dressed nothing like Ken. And something about the way he walked was different. More upright." I shook my head. "I've only seen Ken a few times. I bet the guy I saw just looked a lot like him."

"Well, that simplifies matters," said Rebecca.

"I feel like an idiot for yelling at the poor man, whoever he was," I said, and we both laughed. "Let's do a little shopping. I want to buy gifts for Mom and Doc and Matthew and a few other friends back home."

We ducked into various shops and came back to the inn laden with bags and boxes.

"How about we rest up and then take a walk on the beach?" Rebecca suggested. "The music festival will be going on again tonight. Maybe we can take Penny. You know, to cheer her up a bit."

"Wonderful," I said, yawning as I unlocked the door to my room. "I'll see you in about an hour."

Inside my room, I opened the balcony door to let in the air, stacked my purchases in a corner, and fell into the soft bed. It felt so good to close my eyes. I smiled. Even with all things considered, I was having a wonderful time. I adored my cousins and everything about the island, from the salty air to the roll of the waves and the calls and cackles of the birds.

I should've been out cold within a few minutes, but instead, I tossed around a little bit and finally decided to do a little writing. I was falling behind on my *Dear Miss Smithers* column, and now was the perfect time to answer a few letters and email my responses off to Walter, who'd sent me photos of the latest inquiries the day before. I answered one from a man who wondered if he should add onto his house. Another from a woman who was thinking of writing her life's story and wondering if that was a good idea.

When I read these letters, I liked to make a game of guessing who had sent them. Williamsbridge is a tiny town, and my family has lived there for generations. I knew pretty much everyone. The man considering the home renovation was probably Pete Butler, who had recently purchased a tiny house just off the square— and then had found out his wife was pregnant. With triplets. The woman thinking of writing her memoir was probably Jacki Fentress, a history teacher at Williamsbridge High and the leader of the Write Stuff club. When I read a letter from someone who called herself "Stymied Sister," I guessed it was from Joanne Burk, who was always having conflicts with her sister. Or it might have been from Jaylyn—the aforementioned sister, who was always complaining of conflicts with Joanne. I shook my head and started to type an answer to the question "Sister" had posed.

And then it hit me.

Why hadn't I thought of it before?

CHAPTER 13

"Hi, Rebecca. It's me. Can you meet me in the lobby?" I'd wandered down the stairs and out around the garden paths all the way to the front section of the inn, where the lobby building was located.

"Sure. I'll be right there," Rebecca said with a yawn. "Give me five minutes."

"Bring Penny, okay?"

When Rebecca and Penny arrived in the lobby, I asked Penny to call Ken. "Have him meet us here."

"Sure," said Penny, taking out her phone. "What's this about, Eloise?"

"I have a hunch, but I'm not sure I'm right."

Penny frowned. "He's not picking up his cell phone."

"Try the Bryants' cottage," suggested Rachel. "Do you have that number?"

"Yes," said Penny, scrolling through her contacts and dialing. After a few moments, she shook her head. "He doesn't answer there either."

"We need to find him. He might be in danger," I said. "And we need to go over to the police station and talk to Hayley."

"Good," said Penny. "I've been thinking the same thing." Her cell phone rang.

"Maybe that's Ken," said Rebecca.

"I don't recognize the number." Penny took the call. She looked at Rebecca and me and mouthed the word *Hayley*. Once she got off the phone, she said, "We have to get to the police station right away. You have the keys to the car, Rebecca?"

Rebecca nodded and handed her sister the keys, then she and I jogged to keep up with Penny as she ran for the parking lot.

"Why do you think Ken's in danger?" asked Rebecca as we hurried along.

"I'm probably just being paranoid. I have a feeling that the person who killed Rachel might go after him next." We arrived at the rental car. I jumped into the backseat and Rebecca got into the front and buckled up. Penny was already revving the engine.

"But why—"

Before Rebecca could say more, we'd screeched out of the parking lot and Penny had taken the turn onto Village Street so fast that Rebecca and I were both tossed to the right side of the car.

"Penny, slow down!" said Rebecca.

"Hayley sounded awful. She said her parents sent a lawyer over and they're on their way to the island. She said she needed us to get there right away."

"This is crazy," said Rebecca as she and I flew to the left side of the car on another sharp turn.

We screeched into the parking lot at the station and chased after Penny, who was already throwing open the front door.

There, in the small main room of the station, we found Hayley, standing with Officer Babbish and Detective Bill and a woman in a smart suit who had the definite air of an attorney. Hayley was no longer wearing handcuffs, thankfully, but she still looked pale and worried.

"You just see that you don't leave the island. Okay, young lady?" Officer Babbish said to Hayley.

"She's not going anywhere," said the attorney, stepping protectively in front of Hayley. She gave Babbish and Bill a look of disapproval. "But may I remind you, gentlemen, that the blood on my client's shirt, while it may have belonged to the victim, clearly had nothing to do with the victim's demise. That is circumstantial evidence at best, and it would not be admissible in any court of law. You have no grounds to hold my client, and no grounds to sully the record of an innocent young woman." She narrowed her eyes and to her credit, both Babbish and Bill shrank back a little. "Have I made myself clear?"

There was a beat of stunned silence, and I felt an overwhelming level of respect for this woman—who couldn't have been more than five-foot-two, and yet had the courage of an army. Then Bill nodded and

Babbish mumbled, "Yes, ma'am." The two of them turned and walked back to their desks like school children who'd been reprimanded.

"I'm so glad you're here," said Hayley, hugging Penny, Rebecca, and I in one giant embrace. She turned to her lawyer. "Thank you so much, Ms. Duncroft."

"You can call me Maeve." She held the door open for all of us to exit the building.

Once outside on the sidewalk, Maeve said, "You're free to go, Hayley. If I need anything from you, I'll call. If those two goons bother you, you call me. Understand?"

Hayley nodded. "Do you think they'll arrest me again?"

Maeve shook her head while scribbling something on a notepad. "It's like I said in there, they have no evidence that connects you to the murder. You had blood on your shirt."

"And Rachel was electrocuted," I said. "It never did make sense."

"She wasn't electrocuted," said Maeve, snapping her folio shut and capping her pen.

"What? But—"

"That's what they thought at first because that's what it was supposed to look like," said Maeve, nodding.

"Supposed to look like?" Rebecca said. "So, someone killed Rachel and tried to make it look like—"

"She'd been electrocuted. Yes," said Maeve. "So, everyone would think it was an accident. But the coroner's report told a different story. Rachel was poisoned."

"P—poisoned?" said Penny, swallowing hard. "But how—"

"Cyanide. In the cup of tea she'd been drinking."

"But—"

Maeve's phone rang and she glanced at it. "I've really got to be going. Don't you worry, Hayley. They'll go back to the drawing board and catch the real killer. Worst case, the killer gets away. But either way, you're going to be safe. There's just no real evidence against you."

Hayley nodded and thanked Maeve again, and a moment later, Maeve had taken off down the sidewalk, talking on her phone, her heels clicking briskly on the cobblestones.

"Are you okay?" Penny asked, turning to Hayley.

"I've been better," said Hayley. She began to break down, the tears rolling down her cheeks. She looked at Penny. "We'd just made up, you know. Rachel and me? We'd put it behind us." A sob escaped her. "And now she's gone."

Penny folded her into a warm hug. "Let's get you back to the inn. You need to get cleaned up and eat something. Then we'll talk this out. Okay?"

Hayley nodded gratefully, and we led her to the car.

CHAPTER 14

We took Hayley back to her room—the *Seahorse Suite*—which was on the same floor as Rachel's had been. While she showered and put on clean clothes, Rebecca, Penny, and I went down to the pool, found a shady table, and ordered food for Hayley.

"Her favorite is the chicken salad sandwich with potato chips and fruit," said Penny.

We also tried calling Ken again, but he still didn't pick up. Penny knocked on the door of the Bryant family's cottage, but no one answered.

"He might be out swimming or surfing," said Penny. "He goes out into the water most days. And he always goes out there when he's upset. We could run down and check."

Before we'd made a decision as to whether to make a quick run to the beach, Hayley arrived, looking clean and refreshed, if not a little tired. She brightened when she saw her favorite sandwich waiting for her. "I haven't eaten since yesterday," she said, taking her seat. "I couldn't eat last night, after what happened to Rachel, and then this morning, I was arrested . . . They offered me food at the station, but I'd completely lost my appetite." She picked up the sandwich and took a bite.

"I'm glad to see you feeling up to eating," said Penny.

There was a pause while Hayley chewed and the rest of us tried to figure out a way to begin the discussion.

Finally, I took the lead. "You know, the best way to feel some peace about Rachel and start healing is to figure out who killed her."

Hayley put down her sandwich. "You all believe me, right? I promise I didn't kill Rachel. I was furious at her for dating Ken—that part is true. But I never would have hurt her." She sighed. "I still can't believe this happened when we'd just made up."

"But just think," I said. "What if Rachel had died *before* you'd had a chance to talk it out and forgive each other? As unthinkable as it is that she's gone, at least you can be sure that she knew you loved her."

The other three nodded.

"And I've learned not to hold grudges," said Hayley. "What a waste of time and energy."

"One thing has been bothering me," I said. "I saw you out on the beach yesterday morning. You were having a pretty heated argument with a man." I watched Hayley's face as it clouded over with the memory. "Hayley, I have a hunch about who you were arguing with. But I need you to confirm it."

"It was Ken, right?" asked Rebecca, looking back and forth between me and Hayley in confusion.

Hayley shook her head. "No. It was Ben. Ken's twin brother."

"Ken has a twin brother?" Penny leaned forward, shocked. "How did I not know this?"

"They don't get along. Ben lives in New York and almost never comes around. But he's here now."

"And you'd figured this out, Eloise?" Rebecca asked, looking at me.

"I wasn't sure, but I had a feeling. I'd just answered a letter—" I almost slipped and gave my identity as Miss Smithers away. "I mean, I'd just heard from a couple of sisters back home, Joanne and Jaylyn Burke. They're twins. Then I remembered Ken telling me about his brother and sister when I first met him. And then I remembered looking at the Bryant family photos, over in the lobby. I wondered why Ken and his sister were in the photos, but their brother never was. I mean, even if the brother wasn't nuts about Purple Finch Island, it seemed harsh that he'd be completely excluded from the family photos. Also, when Rebecca and I were in town earlier today, I saw a guy that looked exactly like Ken, but when I called out to him, he didn't answer. So, it finally dawned on me. Ken has an identical twin. The two were never together in those family photos, so it wasn't obvious right away."

"I can't believe this," said Penny. "I mean, Ken's been our guitarist for a while now. I knew he had a brother, but he never brought him around or even talked about him. The one time I asked about him, he just clammed up." She turned to Hayley. "But you knew him? His name is Ben?"

"Well, remember, I dated Ken for three years. I got to know his whole family in that time. Since the brothers weren't on speaking terms, Ken never mentioned him, and I certainly wouldn't have mentioned him either. It would've upset Ken."

"So, what's the deal between them?" asked Rebecca.

"They're identical to look at, but opposites in every other way," said Hayley. "Ken is successful. Ben is a loser."

"How so?" I asked.

"Well, Ken owns a surf shop over on the mainland. The brick and mortar location does very well, but the mail-order component of the business is stellar. He sells surfing equipment all over the world. And he helps manage and maintain Hideaway House here in the summers. Meanwhile, Ben just bounces from one job to another. He never stays in one place long enough to move up. He dropped out of college, while Ken finished with honors."

"Really? Ken?" asked Rebecca.

"Ken is brilliant," said Hayley, nodding. "Don't let his laid-back attitude fool you."

"I had no idea," said Penny.

"He's not one to brag about himself," said Hayley. "That was one of the things I loved about him. And he's charming and romantic and . . . Well, it would be rare to find a woman who could resist Ken. That's why deep down, I understood that Rachel was swept off her feet. I couldn't blame her in the end." She frowned. "But Ben, on the other hand . . . Well, let's just say he didn't have much luck with the ladies. He tries, but he always gets shot down. He dresses well and acts like a hotshot, but once you get to know him a little, you just feel sort of repelled."

"Does Ben have a bad temper?" I asked. "He was really ugly to you on the beach from what I could gather."

Hayley shuddered. "Oh, believe me, you don't want to get on Ben's bad side."

CHAPTER 15

"I don't understand." I tried to keep the compassion in my voice above my confusion. "You know Ken's a suspect in Rachel's murder—just as you have been—and there's a killer on the loose. Why didn't you tell anyone about Ben?"

Hayley looked at me with wide, teary eyes. "I don't know. I think I was in complete shock after what happened to Rachel. And I mean, I knew the guy was a jerk, but it didn't occur to me that . . . Wait. Are you saying you think Ben killed Rachel?"

"Tell me this. What were the two of you arguing about when I saw you on the beach yesterday?"

"I told him he should go away." Hayley took a deep breath and let it out slowly. "He used to cause problems between Ken and me. I was, well, afraid he'd do the same to him and Rachel."

Penny raised a skeptical brow. "Really, Hayley? You were trying to help Ken and Rachel?"

Hayley's face fell.

"Out with it," Penny said.

"You'll think I'm the lowest person ever."

Penny put a hand over her friend's. "Everyone makes mistakes, Hayley. You'll feel better if you tell the whole truth."

Hayley nodded. "Ben wanted to date Rachel. Back when Ken and I were together. He had a huge crush on her. She turned him down. He was sad at first, then furious." She looked from Penny, to me, to Rebecca. "Then obsessed."

"With Rachel?" Rebecca asked.

"Yes. With Rachel. And he was horribly resentful of Ken's ability to win the hearts of women when Ben couldn't. He thought, 'Hey, we're identical twins. If the girls like Ken, they should like me too.'" Hayley shook her head, a look of disgust on her face. "He never understood that real attraction goes deeper than a person's looks."

"So, Ben is a shallow guy," I said.

"Ben is a narcissist," said Hayley. "Anyway, I lied before, when I said I told Ben not to cause problems between Rachel and Ken." A tear rolled down her cheek. "I wanted Ken back. And in my own mind, I thought he'd left me for Rachel, when the truth was, he left me because we weren't good together. Not for the long haul, anyway." She took another deep breath. "Ken left me because our relationship had run its course, and he knew it. And I was just too stubborn or too blind to see it."

"So, when Ben showed up on the island . . ." Penny prompted.

"I knew he still had feelings for Rachel, and I wanted Ken back. Back in New York, Ben had been following Rachel on social media, like a troll. She'd recently posted some photos of her and Ken together, and I think that's what set Ben off. He told me he wanted to break the two of them up, and I went along with that because it could benefit me. He asked me which room she was in and where she hung out . . . And I told him." She put her face in her hands. "I told him where to find her and when. He had a plan to fool her—to let her think he was Ken—and then to let Ken catch her cheating." Hayley looked at me. "I didn't tell people about Ben because I knew the ruse wouldn't work if Rachel knew Ken had a twin. And then later, I *couldn't* tell the police about Ben because that would mean I'd have to confess that I'd acted like a selfish jerk and played a part in his scheme, and that might make them think I could be the killer. I was so set on getting Ken back . . . I was blind to the truth."

"So, yesterday morning, on the beach . . ."

"I had finally realized that Rachel and Ken belonged together. I wanted Ben to go away and leave us all alone. But he wouldn't. He said he was going to make his play for Rachel that evening when she was alone. I told him I'd warn her, but then he said he'd tell her and the whole world how I'd betrayed my friends." Hayley gave Penny an imploring look. "I thought he was going to ask her out again, maybe even try to pass himself off as his brother to get a foot in the door. I swear it never occurred to me that he'd hurt her. I thought he was nuts about her."

I felt my heart beating out of my chest. "I have a very bad feeling that Ben isn't going to stop with Rachel. I think Ken's in danger too."

Hayley nodded. "You might be right, Eloise. I think that when Ben showed up on Purple Finch Island and saw how much in love Rachel was with his brother, he hated them both. He's already killed Rachel. Ken could be next."

"At the very least, he's planning to frame Ken for Rachel's murder," I said.

"We have to stop him!" said Rebecca. "Should we call the police?"

"Definitely," I said. "But we also need to find Ken and warn him." I looked at Hayley. "Can you tell the brothers apart? I mean, I know they dress differently and talk differently. But if Ben was trying to look and act like Ken, is there any way you could tell them apart?"

"Yes."

"How?"

"From a tattoo," said Hayley. "Ken got one on his right shoulder last week. It's a picture of a wave. Ben doesn't even know about it." She scoffed. "It's been driving him nuts that I could tell he was Ben. He couldn't figure out how I was so sure."

"So, you didn't tell him? About the tattoo?"

"No. I'd rather let him squirm."

"Okay. Rebecca, go ahead and call Detective Bill. Meanwhile, let's keep looking for Ken."

"We won't have to look too far," said Penny, standing up suddenly and looking beyond the garden toward the beach. "He's out there in the surf."

CHAPTER 16

"Thank goodness he's okay," said Hayley as we hurried out to the water's edge. "That's got to be Ken. That's his bright orange surfboard."

"Can you see his right shoulder?" I asked.

We all squinted into the bright sunlight, trying to catch sight of the surfer's shoulder. The difficulty of that effort was compounded by the glare of the bright light on the waves, and the fact that the surfer kept falling, then climbing back onto the board and paddling further out.

"You called the police, right, Rebecca?" I asked.

"Yep. They're on the way. I told Detective Bill to look for us out here on the beach in front of Hideaway House."

"Good. Because it looks like our surfer dude just decided he's had enough, and I don't see any tattoo." He was flapping around in the water, trying to turn for the shore, half swimming, half being swept along by the waves.

"Yeah, it's pretty obvious now that that's not Ken," said Hayley. "Ken is at home in the water. Swims like a fish. *This* guy is a mess."

I looked at her. "Hide. *Now*. Ben will know you can identify him and might run. The rest of us will stay here and pretend to believe he's Ken to stall him until the police arrive."

"I don't know about this . . ." said Rebecca. "I'm scared."

I touched her hand. "I am too. But we can't let him get away."

Rebecca gritted her teeth and nodded as Hayley quickly ducked behind a huge hydrangea bush. The rest of us stood our ground next to a towel and duffle bag that most likely belonged to the man in the water, since no one else was around at the moment.

As he got closer to the shore, Ben finally made it to the shallows, where he was able to stand and walk, sputtering and scowling, dragging the surfboard behind him. He spotted us and paused for a split second before coming forward, eyeing us warily, then grabbing the towel at our feet.

He dried himself off. "Rough out there today," he said, looking and sounding for all the world exactly like his brother, save the absence of tattoo.

"Hi, Ken!" I said. "You're really brave to go out in that surf."

"Have a good swim?" asked Penny.

An almost indiscernible wave of relief washed over Ben. "Oh yeah. Gnarly." He glanced at his brother's surfboard. "I'm just off my game a little because—you know." He affected a pained expression.

"Because of Rachel," I finished for him.

He nodded. "Shouldn't have gotten so mad at her, there at the last."

"Mad at her? What are you talking about?" Penny asked.

"I'm ashamed to admit it, but I—well, I got into a big fight with her."

"On Saturday evening?" I asked, beginning to grasp Ben's motive for weaving the tale.

He nodded. "And the guilt is getting to me. I didn't tell the police because I thought they'd figure out—I mean, I thought they'd think I killed Rachel."

I took a step closer to him, playing along with his ploy. "But you didn't, did you, Ken?"

He looked shocked. "Of course not!"

"Good."

"I was just trying to make her sick." His voice was smaller now, his eyes fixed on the ground. "When I took her that tea."

"You put something in her tea," I said.

Ben looked at me in affirmation but said nothing.

"And then you tried to make it look like an accident, with the hair dryer."

"I was so relieved when it turned out the security cameras were on the blink," said Ben. "I thought I was off the hook. But the guilt is getting too heavy to bear."

I tried to will the police to arrive at that moment, but there was still no sign of them. Clearly, Ben had killed Rachel and was now trying to frame his brother. I would've been willing to bet that after planting these deceitful seeds, Ben was planning to hightail it off the island, buy himself an alibi, and let Ken take the heat.

Then the worst possible thing happened. *Ken* came stalking out of the garden toward us.

"Hayley, what are you doing behind that bush?"

Hayley slowly rose from the hydrangeas, her face flushed.

I looked from Ken to his brother, whose eyes had shifted from faux regret to sizzling rage.

Ben looked at Hayley, then at the rest of us, then back at Ken. "What are you doing here?"

"You mean, how did I escape?" Ken glanced at us. "First he knocked me out, then he tied me up, *then* he stuck me in a closet at the cottage and tried to bar the door with a chair." He shook his head at his brother. "And then, apparently, he came out here with my surfboard so that it would appear I was living the highlife without a care in the world. Everyone, meet my brother. Ben."

"He's lying," said Ben, his face clouding over.

"I'm not," said Ken, whipping the right sleeve of his t-shirt up over his shoulder, revealing the tattoo. "Although I don't blame you a bit if you don't want to be *you* at this moment."

Ben eyed the tattoo. "Jerk."

"Loser."

In one very swift movement, Ben scooped up his duffle bag and pulled out a gun. "Not this time I'm not." I was unfortunately standing the closest to him, so he grabbed me and held the gun to my side. "I'd hate to have to kill another of your little girlfriends, brother of mine. But I will if you don't all walk away. *Now.*"

"Leave her alone. Take me—" Ken started to say, but then there was a sickening click as Ben released the safety and pulled back the hammer of the gun.

"Don't hurt her," said Penny, taking a step back. "We'll go."

I felt the barrel of the gun pressing in under my ribcage, felt as if my heart would explode from pounding so hard. *Where were the police?*

Ken put his hands up. "Just stay calm, Ben."

"Don't you tell me to stay calm," said Ben, jamming the gun in further, causing me to flinch.

I looked at Rebecca. The usual sweetness had left her eyes, and her face had hardened, her jaw tightened. She looked like one of those superheroes, transformed and full of grit and courage.

As Hayley, Ken, and Penny started to slowly back away, I heard a sudden, guttural scream as Rebecca lobbed her cell phone at Ben, hitting him squarely in the face. A split second later, she was rushing toward us, crying "No!" and flying at Ben's legs, knocking him to the ground. As if in slow motion, the gun flew out of his hand and I was free. I ran, grabbed the gun, and clicked the safety back on.

"Well done!" Detective Bill and Officer Babbish were running up, a pair of handcuffs gleaming in Officer Babbish's hand.

Within seconds, Ben was cuffed and being led back toward the inn with Ken walking along beside them. Rebecca, Penny, Hayley, and I all hugged.

"That was very brave of you," I said, still amazed at Rebecca's sudden display of courage.

"Yeah, sis," said Penny. "You were fearless!"

"No. I was very afraid." Rebecca looked at me, a smile brightening her sweet face. "But my love for my cousin was bigger than my fear."

Penny grinned and slung an arm around her sister. "I guess you can't be brave if you're not afraid."

CHAPTER 17

"So, Ben pretended to be Ken, took Rachel the poisoned tea, then assumed the security camera footage would hang his brother." I looked at Detective Bill, who was seated with us at a table in the garden that evening. He'd processed Ben, then come back to the inn to take our statements. We were all pretty exhausted, so we were very grateful we wouldn't have to go and sit at the police station all evening.

"That's right," said Bill, leaning back in his chair and folding his hands comfortably over his belly. "He'd been lurking down the hall around the corner when Ken came out of Rachel's room to head over to the concert. He heard Ken call down and order the tea and saw his chance. He met the room service waiter as he was leaving the kitchen and told him he'd make the delivery. The waiter assumed Ben was his brother, of course, so he handed it right over. He fooled Rachel, she drank the tea, and he thought it would be clear to us that Ken was the indisputable killer. After all, we would've seen him intercepting room service, slipping the poison into the tea, and delivering it to Rachel's room on the security footage."

"So then why bother with the whole hairdryer thing?" asked Penny.

Bill nodded. "He confessed that part, too. He wanted it to appear that Ken had killed Rachel and tried to cover it up. Simple as that. Then when Ms. Gander, seeing him and thinking he was Ken, stopped him on his way out and mentioned that she needed to speak with him about the broken security system, he came up with Plan B to frame his brother. He incapacitated Ken, then went out into the surf so people would see him. He'd planned to wait until someone came along so that he could hint at a confession—act like his conscience was getting to him. Then he'd return to the inn, untie his sleeping brother, and leave town."

"When Ken woke up, he'd be a sitting duck," said Rebecca.

"Ben had already gotten his roommate back on the mainland to say he was at home all weekend, so he had a pretty solid alibi," said Bill. "And after all, no one ever sees Ben around the island these days. He had the perfect disguise." He stood and stretched. "But justice has prevailed once again. I'd better be off."

"Wouldn't you like to stay and have a drink?" asked Ken. "Or some dinner? You've been so helpful."

"Sounds nice, but Babbish and I are headed out to the festival tonight. There's a techno rave group playing down the beach."

"*Babbish* listens to techno?" Penny asked.

"Oh, yeah," said Bill. "He's a big fan."

"I'll walk you out," said Ken. "I want to go and check on Jane. I need to make arrangements to get the security system repaired right away."

Bill looked back at us, gave us a little salute and walked off with Ken, his colorful Hawaiian shirt flapping in the breeze.

"I got a call from that talent scout," said Hayley, looking at Penny. "He said he'd like to hear us perform before he heads back over to the mainland. He'll be here for a few more days."

Penny's jaw dropped. "Are you serious?"

"He's seen our video. He said he'd like to give us some pointers," said Hayley. "I thought . . . well, I was hoping you might want to start all over again. From the beginning."

A smile spread across Penny's face. "There's a song in that." She got up and hugged Hayley. "Let's do it."

"And right from the start, let's agree never to date each other's exes. Okay?"

Penny laughed for the first time all day. "Deal."

"We should celebrate," said Rebecca.

"Want to go out?" asked Penny.

"Nope," said Rebecca. "It's been a long day. How about we stay in?"

"Movies and popcorn in our room?" suggested Penny.

"Perfect!" said Rebecca.

"I'm in!" said Hayley, standing.

"You guys go ahead," I said, taking out my phone. "I'm going to call and check in at home, then I'll come up to the room."

They all smiled and walked off, chattering among themselves.

I called Matthew first. I hadn't been able to reach him all day and was aching to hear his voice. My heart sank when he didn't answer. I called Mom next and gave her the highlights of what had happened, bracing myself for her reaction, expecting her to display her usual worry and to encourage me to come home early. But she surprised me by saying, "Eloise, I'm so proud of you."

"You are?"

"Of course, I am." She paused. "Don't get me wrong, I'm horrified that you were in danger. And I wish you were here right now so I could give you a hug. But you've shown yourself to be courageous and capable and extremely perceptive. You have a real mind for solving mysteries." She chuckled. "I can't say I'm surprised by that. You always have been intuitive and curious. Hate to say it, but you'd make a great detective."

I laughed. "I think I'll stick to inn keeping and journalism."

"Good."

"By the way, I can't seem to reach Matthew. Any idea where he is?"

Mom paused. "He's out running an important errand."

"Now? Are you sure?"

Another pause. "I bet you'll hear from him soon."

"Mom, what are you not telling me? Where's Matthew?"

"I'm right here, you silly woman."

I couldn't believe my eyes. Matthew was standing right there, in the flesh, looking a little disheveled, holding a suitcase.

I realized Mom was still on the line. "Mom, he's here!"

"Glad he made it safely. You two have a nice time."

We hung up, and I stood and closed the distance between Matthew and me in a few steps. He swept me into his arms and kissed me.

"I missed you," he said, brushing the hair away from my face.

"I missed you, too," I said. "I can't believe you're here. I thought you needed to stay home and write."

"After the murder mystery weekend came to a close, I tried, but all I was doing was sitting there, staring at my computer screen, thinking about you."

"That's no good."

"Nope."

"But this"—I circled my arms around him and pulled him close—"*this* is good."

"I'm feeling inspired already."

"How long can you stay?"

"The rest of the week. I rented a car and turned it in before the ferry ride over. We can drive back home together in the jeep." He looked around at the beautiful inn and gardens and the sunset over the water beyond. "Although I think I could get used to this."

"It's beautiful, isn't it?"

He touched my cheek. "Not as beautiful as you, El," he said in an almost-whisper.

"Come on, I'll show you around. You need to meet my cousins. Oh—and we have a movie date tonight on the third floor."

Matthew laughed. "Good, because after rushing across Vermont, New Hampshire, and Maine, I'm pooped."

I took his hand and led him toward the building. "You came all that way, just to see me."

"I'd go further than that to see the love of my life," he said.

I stopped and turned back to him. I could feel my cheeks burning and didn't even care. "Did I mention I love you?"

"I love you, too." He grinned. "It's nice, saying it in person."

"Best thing I ever heard."

"I thought you said the best thing you ever heard was the printing press churning out the newspapers at the *Onlooker*."

"You know me so well." I laughed and pulled open the door. "But not as well as I know you."

"You think?"

"I'm positive."

"We'll see about that."

"Sounds like a challenge."

"I love a challenge." He kissed my hand and followed me up the stairs. "You're on."

THE INN AT PUMPKIN HILL'S PUFFED PANCAKE

(This recipe makes one pancake the size of a pie pan—approximately two servings. At the inn, we often bake two at a time—especially if Matthew and Doc are coming to breakfast.)

2 T butter

2 eggs

½ cup flour

½ cup milk

¼ t salt

½ t almond extract

THE INN AT PUMPKIN HILL'S PUFFED PANCAKE

Toppings: berries, sliced fruit, powdered sugar, maple syrup, honey, whipped cream—whatever you'd like!

Preheat the oven to 400 degrees and adjust the racks into the lower section so that the pancake will have plenty of room to rise. Put the butter into a pie pan and put it into the oven. Leave it in until the butter is melted and hot—but be careful that it doesn't burn. Meanwhile, mix together the eggs, flour, milk, salt, and almond extract. When the butter is ready, carefully take it out of the oven and immediately pour the batter into the pan. Then slip the pan back into the oven. Bake for 20 minutes, or until the pancake is puffed up and golden brown. Remove from oven and fill with berries, a sprinkle of powdered sugar, and a drizzle of maple syrup or honey. Also delicious with sliced peaches. Or add a squirt of whipped cream and sprinkles for a fun dessert! Slice and serve warm from the oven.

AUTHOR'S NOTE

I'd love to hear your thoughts on my books, the storylines, and anything else that you'd like to comment on —reader feedback is very important to me. My contact information, along with some other helpful links, is listed on the next page. If you'd like to be on my list of "folks to contact" with updates, release and sales notifications, etc.… just shoot me an email and let me know. Thanks for reading!

Also…

… if you're looking for more great reads, Summer Prescott Books publishes several popular series by outstanding Cozy Mystery authors.

CONTACT SUMMER PRESCOTT BOOKS PUBLISHING

Twitter: @summerprescott1

Bookbub: https://www.bookbub.com/authors/summer-prescott

Blog and Book Catalog: http://summerprescottbooks.com

Email: summer.prescott.cozies@gmail.com

YouTube: https://www.youtube.com/channel/UCngKNUkDdWuQ5k7-Vkfrp6A

And…be sure to check out the Summer Prescott Cozy Mysteries fan page and Summer Prescott Books Publishing Page on Facebook – let's be friends!

CONTACT SUMMER PRESCOTT BOOKS PUBLISHING

To download a free book, and sign up for our fun and exciting newsletter, which will give you opportunities to win prizes and swag, enter contests, and be the first to know about New Releases, click here: http://summerprescottbooks.com

Printed in Great Britain
by Amazon